Magic

The circus tent was glowing pale in the rain like a fleshy flower lit from within. It seemed to bloom in the downpour. Drops of rain caught on Rafe's eyelashes, blinding him as the circus lights struck them. He groped for the flap, that slit in the fabric that would reveal her to him.

She was on the rope again, her skirt flashing with tiny mirrors, hair braided with petals. He looked up at her, dizzy with it, seeing her face framed in the parasol. There were bluish shadows around her eyes.

A centaur galloped in circles around the ring, his man's head and torso straining awkwardly against the force of his thick, shuddering haunches. Another creature, a bitter-lipped, bare-breasted woman with the lower body and legs of a peacock, strutted back and forth in a circle of light, juggling. These half-human creatures, strange mutations—all that was left of the animals in Elysia. Rafe hardly noticed them. Only the girl walking above, the girl Calliope had visioned, the girl he had been watching for weeks now.

FIREBIRD
WHERE FANTASY TAKES FLIGHT™

Ecstasia

Francesca Lia Block

FIREBIRD

AN IMPRINT OF PENGUIN GROUP (USA) INC.

FIREBIRD

Published by Penguin Group

Penguin Group (USA) Inc., 345 Hudson Street, New York, New York 10014, U.S.A.

Penguin Books Ltd, 80 Strand, London WC2R ORL, England

Penguin Books Australia Ltd, 250 Camberwell Road, Camberwell, Victoria 3124, Australia

Penguin Books Canada Ltd, 10 Alcorn Avenue, Toronto, Ontario, Canada M4V 3B2

Penguin Books (N.Z.) Ltd, 182-190 Wairau Road, Auckland 10, New Zealand

First published in the United States of America by Roc,
an imprint of New American Library, a division of Penguin Books USA Inc., 1993
Published by Firebird, an imprint of Penguin Group (USA) Inc., 2004

1 3 5 7 9 10 8 6 4 2

THE LIBRARY OF CONGRESS HAS CATALOGED THE ROC EDITION AS FOLLOWS:

Block, Francesca Lia.

Ecstasia / by Francesca Lia Block.

p. cm.

ISBN 0-451-45280-7

I. Title.

PS3552.L617E28   1993

813',54—dc20   92-42772

CIP

ISBN 0-14-240037-8

Printed in the United States of America

For Christopher Schelling,
and for
Fred Drake, who made the desert bloom

Ecstasia

PART 1

Orpheus

UNDERGROUND

Once I had a dream
She woke me from my sleep
Taught me to believe
Now I've lost her in a nightmare
But I'm going to find her somewhere
Even if it takes me Under
Even if it takes me down
Under underground

Here above the ground
Ferris wheels go round
And the dance of clowns
A carnival—this town
Only a playground
Stay young, stay up above
Before it takes you down
Underground

Underground 1

CALLIOPE'S VISION

The girl is floating above. Folding out from her thin, white back are wings. They are dusted with pollen like poppies. They have veiny eyes, meant to terrify predators. The girl floats on these wings, always just out of reach.

She remembers—in her bones and blood, for she has never seen them—she remembers when there were others—smaller, all wings, like flowers lifted from their stems. Their eyes did not protect them. She remembers, in a dream, flowers growing from the earth.

Beneath her, the boy drifts in a river. He is a river. His hair is shiny black ripples. His eyes are bright, wet reflections. His limbs flow. He is the song. Like the river he sings.

And always, above him, the wings hover. As the sunlight shines through, they are like stained glass, casting their rainbows on the river. The river that travels through the desert, toward a place where horses will join it, where swans will join it and lilies grow on its banks, where there will be green again, as there was once.

The river-boy will join a body of water, his song becoming part of a chorus. The winged girl will dance above him. He will rise from the water and walk on his legs. She will alight beside him. Her vast wings will leave her, becoming other, smaller pairs of wings.

The desert will green once again.

The boy sitting on the curb in front of the circus tent looked as if he had come from the sea. His cheekbones were like pale half-shells and his hair was so black it seemed wet. Around him, streetlights, like reflections in dark water, blurred in the moist air.

The girl walking the tightrope seemed more air than any other element. Through the flaps of the tent, the boy could see her balancing, lights flickering on the net skirt she wore. She was almost unnaturally thin.

The boy beat on the drum in his lap, his veins filling with blood, becoming taut as the line she walked.

Finally, he pulled the pocket watch out from inside his shirt. It was heavy in his hand, the tiny silver drum his mother had given him, and he sighed. He was already late. Looking back at the girl, he drew up his hood and ran through the narrow, cobbled streets of Elysia.

People were out tonight, on their way to dance clubs and

diners, dressed in their feathers and lights and lace, protected from the rain by beaded umbrellas or massive hats shaped like clouds and stars. He dodged among them.

The carnival yard was almost deserted now, but the Ferris wheel revolved, casting light like a planet for a sky that offered only darkness and toxic drizzle. The boy passed a glass building where a mechanical doll with clocks set in her eye sockets served fluorescent drinks. The doll's head swiveled, and she stared at him through the sparkling walls; he turned from her gaze.

He crossed the street, unlocked the door of the loft, and bounded upstairs. The music was sifting down to meet him and he could almost see it—like some metallic pollen floating on the air.

Murals of ornate silver gardens were painted on the high, angled walls of the room. Huge oval mirrors in frames of silver roses reflected the tapestry cushions and the urns holding bright candy, thick chalky sticks of burning incense or transparent silk blossoms. And there were the instruments.

The musicians stopped playing when the boy, Rafe, entered. Paul looked up from his massive guitar, his eyes pale, startling fire in his scarred face. The lights of the Ferris wheel shone in on him through the window.

"Where've you been?"

Rafe sat at his drum set, twirling the sticks in his hands. He looked at his sister Calliope who stood with her fingers poised above the keyboards. Her broad face comforted the way their mother's face had once eased the panic that beat in him.

Dionisio put down his bass and tilted back his head, swallowing the chocolate-mint liqueur from a bottle, licking his lips.

"So who is she?"

"What?"

"Who is she? This wild creature you've been hunting."

"There's no one. You only think of one thing, Dionisio. Maybe I'm just busy."

"Busy making love. I can see in your eyes, boy."

It was Calliope's eyes that changed then. "Dino, maybe Rafe's been working. Some people do that."

"My baby-girl, I just think he should share this with us," Dionisio said. "It might be inspiring. We could write a song." His nostrils flared. "And last night, Callie had one of her visions of you with a beauty. She was tiny and dark and she could float."

Rafe looked at his hands. Calliope knew. Callie always knew. She had seen things before they happened since they were children.

"Why don't we forget about Rafe's sex life?" Paul said. His voice was sharp. "You especially, Rafe. And put some of that energy into the music. We have a lot of shows coming up, and I can't do this by myself. Between you being late and Dino's drinking . . ."

"Paul . . ."

"Listen, Callie, stop trying to defend your baby brother so much. He has to grow up."

"I think we could all use some of that, not just Rafe. Everyone acts like children around here."

Dionisio laughed. "Of course. We'll start wanting to go Under if we grow up. Better stay crazy-boys like Rafe."

Rafe flipped the drumsticks in the air. Here they were, talking about this again. He didn't understand it. That they would go underground willingly as soon as lines began to show on their faces. That they would go the way everyone went, the way his mother had gone. He saw Estrella's eyes, the deep lines around them giving her a constant smile. Still, he could not imagine her underground. Her image had nothing to do with that place, that darkness.

"I'm not going to go. No one forces us."

Paul turned to him, his face beautiful in its angularity, even with the scars on his cheeks. "You'll go," he said. "Everyone goes. How would you like to be the only old face around here? Everyone perfect and you're this ruin. You'll go down."

"It's the price you pay, boy," said Dionisio. "For all the pleasures of this playground town. So you'd better take them now. It's the price you pay, just like your mama did. You know that."

Rafe drummed lightly on the skin of the bass drum. He wondered sometimes what he would do if he didn't play music, where the energy would go in his body. Would there be some kind of explosion?

Yes, his mother had paid. She had left the desert where no one goes Under, where the old ones live until they die. She had wanted something, some sweetness—to paint herself like an opal, eat cakes, to dance all day. And she had wanted that for her children, too. But the pleasures of Elysia did come with a price. Underground, the old ones, disintegrating to powder, shuffled through tunneling streets; the addicts huddled in their dealer's doorways, flesh peeling to ash.

"I wish she never came here. She should have stayed in the desert."

"And miss all the fun?" Dionisio said. He was smiling but his mouth looked bitter.

Calliope touched her temples. "Can we just play some music?"

"See you all Under." Dionisio finished the last drop in his bottle.

"Not me," said Rafe.

"The lines are starting to show already, boy."

"Yours, Dino." Rafe began to play.

The music was penetrating, filling the loft like smoke, and Paul, his voice an ice fire, sang:

"Under underground . . ."

If you had been able to ask any of them while they were playing, while they were Ecstasia, if you had asked what wounded them or even what they wanted, they would have not been able to answer. They knew only that this thing was happening between them, and they let themselves dissolve into it like one melts into the body of a lover after years of separation or an ancient ritual in a world where faith has been forgotten. They did not know what it could do for anyone else, but while they were playing, Ecstasia became their oasis and their temple.

They forgot their anger and desire. Only afterwards, when the song was over, did they wish that it could have gone on forever.

⌒

Rafe left the loft. It was raining harder now, and people hurried through the streets, heads down, to find shelter in perfumed rooms from the chemical stench of the water.

The circus tent was glowing pale in the rain like a fleshy flower lit from within. It seemed to bloom in the downpour. Drops of rain caught on Rafe's eyelashes, blinding him as the circus lights struck them. He groped for the flap, that slit in the fabric that would reveal her to him.

She was on the rope again, her skirt flashing with tiny mirrors, hair braided with petals. He looked up at her, dizzy with it, seeing her face framed in the parasol. There were bluish shadows around her eyes.

A centaur galloped in circles around the ring, his man's head and torso straining awkwardly against the force of his thick, shuddering haunches. Another creature, a bitter-lipped, bare-breasted woman with the lower body and legs of a peacock, strutted back and forth in a circle of light, juggling. These half-human creatures, strange mutations—all that was left of the animals in Elysia. Rafe hardly noticed them. Only the girl walking above, the girl Calliope had seen in a vision, the girl he had been watching for weeks now.

She came down and stretched her tiny arms and legs. He imagined circling her upper arm with his fingers. She turned and looked at him.

"Where'd you learn that?" he asked before he could think about it. He moved nearer.

"I've been tightrope walking since before I could walk." Her voice was breathy.

"What's it like?"

"Like floating in air, but you have to know about the earth, too."

"You're amazing."

She thanked him. Then something behind him caught her eye and he turned to see. An old one dressed in a clown suit with a petalled collar, rode past on a unicycle. It was rare to see old ones above still, and Rafe felt his stomach clench. Even for a circus freak, this man shocked him. He was amazed that anyone could stay above looking like this, taking the abuse.

"Who is that?" Rafe asked the girl.

"The Old Clown." Her eyes were soft, watching the man.

"Why's he still up here?"

"He doesn't want to go down. He thinks he should live as long as he's alive. But people are cruel."

"Why doesn't he go to the desert?" Rafe asked. "No one would bother him there."

They both turned to see the clown wheeling around the tent, a strange smile on his withered face.

"He says he's addicted to Elysia. To all the sugar-things. He's a sugar-head," the girl said. Then she turned to Rafe. "I've heard it's so dark in the desert."

"My mother said you can see stars there."

The girl looked up at the clusters of crystalline lights suspended above the circus ring. "I've never seen them."

Rafe remembered his mother pointing to the sky. "In the desert there aren't all these bright lights or fumes," she had said as they stood among the pink flashes and blue fires of Elysia. "You can see the stars." It was one of the few times Rafe remembered having heard regret in her voice. Then she added quickly, "They don't look like much. Small, pale lights."

"I'm not going Under, are you?" Rafe heard himself asking. His voice was urgent and he seemed surprised at the question.

"I ask everybody. I think about it all the time. I'm not going."

"I am. I'm going," she said. "I'm afraid to stay up here. People hurting you all the time when you start to age. Mirrors everywhere, reminding you. Showing lines and old flesh. I'm not as brave as the Old Clown."

"But you could go to the desert." He looked at her. The blue shadows reminded him of tears being held back, pressed beneath the skin.

"It's too dark at night. Even with stars. It's just rock and sand and heat. And what if you got sick? Here, if you get sick, there's a place to go right away."

Under. A bed in the sick-rooms, Rafe thought. "There's no light down there at all. No stars, even, nothing. Haven't you heard that?" He had dreamed of the darkness beneath him sometimes—awakened sweating with the nightmare of it, torn back the covers so the electric carnival lights of Elysia shone in on him again through the windows of the loft.

"If I were sick, I wouldn't want light. Just a place to hide."

"Why do you even think about that?" he asked. "How could you want to go Under at all?" Again, the urgency. The panic. He breathed in sharply. He hadn't meant to frighten her. She was so exquisite—her pallor, the flowers lit in her hair.

Her voice was different when she spoke again. "I don't want it. But I accept it. I enjoy my life now. But when the time comes, I'll go. Like everyone else." She started to turn away.

Rafe knew he should stop. But he felt as if he were arguing with himself—the need to escape Elysia and the fear. "You could keep enjoying your life."

"You talk too much," she said. "I don't even know you." She seemed surprised that she had been drawn into this exchange at all, angry.

He had not meant to say any of this. He had only meant to . . . "I'm sorry. I'm Rafe. You're . . ."

"Lily."

She looked back at him from the tear-shadows before she disappeared behind a glittery, rose-colored curtain.

ESTRELLA'S LETTER

My children,

I am writing to you so that when I am Under, you will have something to hold in your hands, something that will not age, ruin, vanish. I want you to remember everything that was bright and sweet about our time together. I need you to remember so that it will remain real.

And do not think of where I have gone.

Once, I lived in the desert. The sands blew, parching my eyes and throat. I worked all day among the skull rocks, trying to make the cracked earth yield something green. I dreamed of flowers—I had heard tales of mute creatures shaped like stars that came up from the ground, featureless faces, colors I hardly believed in. Sometimes, when the heart sizzled, I saw them—these flowers—burning in the distance, a shimmer of green and the startling cool sheen of water. This is what my children will have, I told myself. But they will not just see it beckoning before them while their throats ache with dryness. The water will shine over their bodies, will fill their mouths. They will lose themselves in flowers and eat fruits that drop into their hands. They will spend their days performing on a stage of meadow grasses, behind curtains of willow trees, surrounded by the white swans, horses, wildcats, and butterflies like loosened flowers—all these that are only stories now. That is where my children belong. They will have everything.

That is what I thought, blinking into the searing sun while the island of green floated away from me. But the island was never real. There is nowhere I know of like that desert dream. Instead, I heard tales of another place.

A dark place. But lit. Lit with different, brighter, nearer stars. Not a green place, but there were flowers grown in houses of green glass and manufactured mist. No birds but feathers, the most dazzling plumage. And stages, yes, different from the ones I imagined for you—gilded, lined with columns in rooms full of murals and mirrors. Carved horses, billowing tents, strobe lights, fireworks, cakes and all the faces beautiful—beautiful as the flowers in my mirage. This is the new mirage—one that we can touch, we can smell and taste and hear—the music of it—one that we can enter. We can enter. The city called Elysia.

It was your father who brought me there. He came to the desert one day, bringing potions, elixirs to heal the body and the mind. Everyone gathered around his ancient, finned, dust-caked car, seeking the small glass vials filled with essences that would cool the burn of the sun, ease the ache in their muscles, dissolve the screams straining in their throats. When he drew back the hood of his cloak, I recognized him. I had dreamed of a man running along the dunes, unrolling a bolt of cloth. The cloth kept changing—silver stars on sky silk, liquid velvet rainbows, jewel-encrusted cobweb lace, thick embroidered roses. I did not know the name for these things when I had that dream—silk, velvet, lace, roses. And I did not know the name of the man who ran, laughing as he spread that path of color on the sand. But I learned all the names.

Your father did not carry a bolt of cloth, but when he took my hands and looked into my eyes, I saw the dream-fabrics that I ached to touch.

"You come from there," I said. "What is it like? Why did you leave?"

He frowned and stared across the dunes. Already, lines had begun to form around his eyes, but I did not notice things like that then. "It is no place to live," he told me. "As soon as you grow old . . ."

"But look around you," I said. "Is this any life? Burning up out here without any beauty to sustain us. I must find somewhere else."

"Not there," he said.

I got up and went to my tent. He stood alone, kicking dust on the remains of the fire beneath the stars.

The next morning, when I rose to hunt for lizards, I found something outside my tent. It was a silk rose. I pressed it to my skin between my breasts where the sun hadn't toughened me. Nothing that soft had ever touched me. What would it be like to wear an entire dress like that, touching me everywhere, to see a room full of those flowers? I knew it was from him and that he had brought it with him from there, from Elysia.

When I found him, he looked as if he hadn't slept. I thanked him and asked about the real roses.

"They grow in green glass houses. And they smell like . . ."

"I wouldn't know anything you compare them to," I said.

"Do you know what happens there?" he asked.

I had heard the tales.

"Yes, you will have rich things to eat and drink, silks to wear, flowers, dancing," he said. "I know how tempting it is. It drew me to it, dazed, fluttering. Knocking myself against those sparkling glass windows to get inside to the champagne and the champagne-colored light. But it is very brief. As soon as you begin to age, you will go down below. To the other place. No one will force you. But you will see your reflection in a mirror—a few lines, a pallor, a weakness in the curve of your shoulders and back. And you will go. Your own face will suddenly disgust you and you will go below. To Under. There you will not have to see your face. It is so dark and there are no mirrors. You will see your face reflected only in the faces of others——the old ones like you. There will no longer be any sweet brightness, any of the things you came to Elysia for. There will no longer be any light at all. Then you will remember the desert. You will remember desert light, clear and pure. You may remember people's voices singing around a fire in the night. You may remember the taste of food you brought from the dry earth, coaxed from impossibly dry earth with your own hands and the salt of your body. You may, if your mind is still clear enough, remember stars. And you will wish for the desert then. Where no one judges your face or your spine. But it will be too late."

I hardly heard him. I was thinking of a shower of roses falling on us, real ones with scent. And I was thinking of him holding me in his arms while the flowers fell around us and mirrors reflected our young bodies again and again.

Later, he gave me the gift of the dream, but it was not in the same form. Instead of that fabric, he gave me you, Calliope and Rafe. My path of constellations, water, and petals. After both of your births, I lay in the heat of the tent, looking through the flap at the green mirage swimming in the distance, thirsting for it. I imagined that you both saw it, too, and held out your tiny hands. Your father came into the tent, stooping, covered with dust. His eyes were my oasis, my healing tonic. He quenched my thirst. "My garden," he called me.

"How can I take you there? Even if I weren't afraid for myself? How can I let you go down before your life is half over? Estrella."

"So instead I will die without ever knowing it," I said. "Is that what you are saying? And our children. You were strong enough to leave. You enjoyed it and then you left. Why can't we do that again?"

"Look at me, Estrella. If I go back, I will have to go down."

"No!" I said. "We have plenty of time. Then we will leave and come back here." He was so beautiful to me. I saw his thick hair and broad back and I was not afraid. When he smiled, he looked like a young child. I did not understand then.

"I thought I had left that place forever." He stroked the hair off of my hot forehead and I knew then that I had won, that he would lead me away from the rocks shaped like skulls and limb bones, lead me to my mirage.

❧

I imagined that there would be gates with sentinels who stripped us of our clothes and examined our faces and bodies for signs of age. There was nothing like that. I did not know then that our sentinels would awaken within us as soon as we entered this place. There was only a cluster of lit buildings in the midst of an expanse of night. We could hear music as we approached, nothing like the simple tin bells and drums in the desert. This music was flashing and metal-bright. I started dancing in my seat with you, Rafe, in my arms. You were just a tiny baby, but when you heard the music and saw the lights you started shivering. Your whole body trembled. I took your hand,

Calliope, and you wanted to dance, too. I thought you would sprout wings. And when your father saw us like that, covering his face and throat and hands with kisses, the worry left his face. He looked even younger to me then, and I was not afraid of anything. At that moment, we would be young forever.

We were so happy. I knew I had made the right choice. Everything I had dreamed of was real. A dress of roses. A hall of mirrors. Chiming silver clocks. A piano. I held Rafe's hands in mine and touched his fingers to the keys. Rafe, you never stopped moving. You were a musician already. You both were! Calliope, you loved that piano. We lit candles and placed them on it. Their flames were reflected in the rosy polished wood. Your father and I drank plum liqueur, and we watched the fireworks through the glass doors while Calliope played.

Then your father began to change. He stopped working in his laboratory, finding secret cures. He stood before the mirrors looking at his face.

I tried to soothe him, but his shoulder jerked away. "You are still a young man," I said.

"I am a desert, Estrella."

He grew more and more furious at his face. Perhaps I should have packed what I could, put all of you in the car, and begun the journey back to the desert. But I could not see what was happening, or I did not want to see. I did not want to leave our new, rich life.

Forgive me, Rafe. Perhaps I could have prevented that night. After, you ran away. Calliope and I drove through the streets calling your name. The dark cobblestone streets seemed to wind forever, leading nowhere. Finally, Callie and I found ourselves at the edge of Elysia, at the edge of the lights. I was afraid to move back out into the dark desert. It was you, Callie, with your visions, who pointed forward, across the dunes. The lights of Elysia were just a haze. Calliope told me to stop, and we got out of the car. The dry wind drew the moisture from our eyes and lips. I was almost blind, but Calliope's steps were sure, pressing forward over the slipping sand that kept drawing us back.

Rafe. You were lying in a dark and shifting bank of sand, whispering to yourself. I lifted you in my arms. Calliope held my hand. Our shadow was like a huge, strange beast crossing the desert.

Your father looked up only for a moment. The landscape of his face in the candlelight reminded me of a harsher desert than the one we had come from. Suddenly, I realized I would rather have stayed forever out in the dunes than hide in the hollows of that face. The real desert had mirages hidden in it, a moon.

Something had happened to him.

"We must leave here," I said. "When it is light, we will go back."

All night I sat up with both of you among the flowers in the greenhouse, singing, letting the moisture return to our flesh. Rafe trembled, as if flames of pain were still kindling on his back. Finally, he fell asleep in my arms.

The next morning, your father was gone. He left these words:

"I saw what I had become—an old man—and I lost all power

over myself. How could my hands wound what I love most? Once I believed that my hands could find cures.

"I do not want to take you away from your lives here. And even if we went back to the desert, Estrella, maybe it is too late. I will never know for sure if the fury will return. Please forgive me, my beloved Estrella, Calliope, and Rafe. My son, please forgive me for harming you."

He had gone Under.

I decided we would remain in Elysia so that you could continue to have its gifts. I made you costumes—magicians' top hats, starry cloaks—and taught you the dance steps and rhythms I knew. Then you taught yourselves. I believe that the music, the dancing, the magic tricks are the things that heal us. They transform the air and our lives. You transformed my life, there on the dais I had built in our living room, wearing your hats full of velvet rabbits and fluttering paper flowers. I knew it was worth the loss, to come to Elysia for these moments, seeing my children in their oasis of sound and motion. In the desert, you would have been able to play simple instruments and dance on the sand, but the winds would rip your music away. The sand would burn through your sandals. You would not be clothed in iridescence.

Remember, when I have gone Under, that these moments of youth, glittering on stage, moving your audience to sweat and tears, are worth a great loss. Do not think of me or of the time when you, too, decide to leave Elysia. Give your spirits to your music and give your music to the air as if it were moisture from flowers; give your music to the earth as if it were the light of the sun. And if you play beautifully, I may feel it through the earth. I may hear you from underground and lift my face up, able to imagine stars.

With all my love,

Your mother

Calliope fingered the letter, its ink smudged and fading, the delicate paper creased. Years had passed. Soon, even this last message from Estrella would disintegrate entirely.

Whenever she saw flowers, Calliope thought of her mother. She imagined that her touch could make them grow, that if, somehow, Estrella returned to her children, to Elysia, she would bring with her some magic potion that would make seeds unfurl green in the earth, reaching up through the dry soil to the sky without artificial temperature or light, without houses of glass. Enough blossoms and green would grow that Estrella, Rafe, Paulo, Dionisio, and Calliope could leave Elysia and plant their own oasis in the desert. Estrella would bring the secrets of plants and waterfalls and streams with her from underground.

Calliope could close her eyes and see her mother, laughing, walking up through the tunnel that led back to Elysia with a miniature, tree-covered green island in her hands. Estrella held out the island like a bouquet. Calliope and Rafe ran to meet her. She looked just the same as when she had left them.

But this picture in Calliope's mind was not one of her visions. It was only a fantasy, a dream. She wished for a vision that would lead her to Estrella.

She remembered. Waking that morning at dawn, years ago. At that time in her life she had not learned to believe in her visions, although they had guided her fingers on the piano keys and even helped her and Estrella find Rafe in the dunes. So that morning, when she saw in her mind the image of Estrella, opalescent, wrapped in a long cloak, fleeing through the streets of Elysia toward the gaping tunnel, she only tried to blink it away. She was not terrified. It did not seem real.

"Mama!" she had called, but there was silence in the apartment. Rafe was sleeping in the next bed. Calliope remembered thinking how young and small he looked. She leaped up and ran barefoot into Estrella's room. The bed was made. There was a jar of greenhouse roses beside it. She ran into the living room, through the rest of the apartment. Each room was empty. Before her eyes was the misty vision of her mother running.

Calliope started to rush out the front door but remembered her sleeping brother and came back. That was when she found the letter on her bedside table, beneath the silk rose her father had given her mother when they had first met in the desert.

"And do not think of where I have gone," Estrella's letter said.

Rafe woke to the sound of Calliope's sobs. "Mama!" he cried, imitating her. She held him in her arms and held back her tears. This is what everyone did, the price they paid, she told herself, watching the jewel-colored lights flicker in the streets. But inside of Calliope, her tears remained, cherished tenderly, like a child she must always protect.

And the tears were still there tonight, years later. Finally,

Calliope let them come into the light as she held the letter in her hands; she knew she had waited long enough.

CALLIOPE'S VISION

At first I see the flower. It grows, impossibly, between cobblestones, without green glass around it. I stoop to touch this impossible flower. That is when the cobblestones begin to slide, the pavement cracks, the earth opens, steam rises from the chasm, and I can see further than I have ever seen before. Down.

The room is full of smoke. It clears in places and there are the bodies, lying on cots, their limbs wrapped in strips of white linen. I know that they are decaying slowly beneath those wraps. All that can be seen are eyes. Finally, I find her eyes—hardly recognizable anymore, peering out from the linen mask. But they are her eyes.

"Calliope," she whispers. "My daughter, there are no gardens. My whole life I have looked for gardens. Now I dream of them, but I can't see them in the dreams. Only a foliage of sewer steam and shadow. What do they smell like? I cannot even remember our greenhouse. If only I could sit in a greenhouse breathing petals and pollen before I die. Just a moment of that. Calliope, what do you remember? Did you see my mirage in the desert? Did you see when I pointed through the flaps of our tent?"

"Where do I begin?"

"I always told you to forget. But now I need you, Calliope. Will you come to me just once? Even if I cannot come back up with you to die there. If I see your face, it will be enough. Your face is the flower I dream of, obscured by shadow in my dream. Come to me and lift your veil, unbind the linen from my hands, so that I will be able to touch you, Calliope, before I die here."

"Mother, where do I begin?"

"The tunnel. You know that is the way. You will light this place."

⁓

"Rafe, I had one of my visions. It was her."

"You saw her?"

"Under. She wanted me to go to her."

"Calliope!"

"Just to say goodbye. She is dying, Rafe."

"You can't go down there."

"She used to sing to us in the greenhouse. Remember?"

He shrugged.

"And when we got out of the bath she held up the towel. 'Come on wings of love to me, my Hercules,' she said, wrapping us in the towel. Remember?"

"I was really young then."

"Will you go with me?"

"We can't go down. I never believed she should have left when she did, but there's nothing we can do, especially now. It's been years, Calliope. I thought you'd accepted it."

"I did until I saw her face and I heard her calling me. We don't have much time."

"Promise me you won't go. Promise me!"

Calliope turned away from Rafe, and he grabbed her arm, pulling her back.

"But I saw her eyes."

"She's gone. Promise me, Callie."

She leaned her head on her brother's shoulder but did not answer him.

⌒

Dionisio was poured out on the black divan. Two girls wearing animal-print dresses sat on either side of him, fondling his curls and taking sips from the huge bottle he held.

"Where's my sister?"

When he saw Rafe, Dionisio tried to sit up. His gaze and speech were moist, blurred.

"Hey, Rafe-boy. I don't know. I tried to stop her. There were so many people . . ." He gestured around the room, confused, then remembered the girls and tried to extricate himself from them. One pulled him back.

"Where's Paul?"

Dionisio pointed a shaky finger at Paul's door just as it opened.

"What's going on?" Rafe asked Paul. "Where's Calliope?"

"Where were you?"

"Just driving around, thinking. Who cares? I wasn't up for a party. But I expect you both to be more aware of what happens to my sister."

"What's with you?"

"Paul, Calliope's going through something. And it doesn't

help to see her lover with two girls in her own house. You're the one that's acting different."

"You're so busy with your new girlfriend I'm surprised you notice anything."

"She's not my girlfriend. I just saw some girl in the tent. Calliope's visions aren't necessarily fact. And so what anyway, Paul?" He looked at the girls with Dionisio. "Can you get them out of here?"

Paul walked slowly toward the couch and stood staring down at the girls, not blinking. They squirmed and stood up, reaching for their wraps. Dionisio collapsed into the pillows.

"Calliope," Dionisio murmured. "My baby-girl . . ."

Rafe glared at him, then made his way through the strewn cups, bottles, confetti, balloons, and trampled paper streamers to his room. He felt safer there, in the embrace of the fawn-colored, curved suede walls, under the stars. He and Calliope had painted them on the ceiling over the drum-shaped bed after a watercolor sketch their mother had made.

Their mother. Rafe reached for the piece of paper lying on the bed. It was the letter from Estrella—the only sign Calliope had left him.

DIONISIO'S DRINK

Calliope, my lynx-girl, I see you in this glass. But where are you? I didn't mean to mess you up. Those girls were a ruin—I lost control. And I had been drinking too much again. Seems like that's all there is to do here sometimes, Miss Girl, why is that? I want your body beside mine in the bed. I can't sleep without you. Where did you go? I'm thinking of you so strong. When we met, you had those grapes and leaves in your hair and you were riding the carousel wild cat—no horse for you—tilting back your head. I can see your thirsty throat. We danced all night like wild things. We knew already then. I whispered that I wanted to see you. So you went into the lounge and came out with your chest heaving, a different scent than before, something crumpled in one hand, and you held your coat closed with the other. I hadn't expected that from you. You had the most spiritual face. I didn't understand what spirit meant, maybe. Maybe I still don't. You are my teacher. But that night we were standing there in the dark corridor and you handed me the crumpled fabric—it was the dress you had been wearing. I pressed it to my neck and you let the jacket fall open and I saw you so perfect I felt I had found the moon—a moon as bright and smooth up close as it looks from far below. You taste better than all the wines. You taste like crystal nectar. And you glow like wine in glass. You cool me out. Our music is our bodies melding and blending, flowing and peaking and ebbing. Why didn't you tell me where you were going, Calliope?

With his hand drum strapped over his shoulders, Rafe stood at the throat of the tunnel. Cold, metallic air and darkness blew up from its belly.

Years before, Rafe's father had gone Under through this tunnel. Rafe hardly remembered him—only a shadowy face repeated in mirrors, a hand flashing, a vague wincing pain on

Rafe's back and thighs. After his father had gone, Rafe never stared into the tunnel, seeking a sign of him, wondering if the man were still alive down there.

But when Estrella left . . .

Every time Rafe passed the entrance he would look down, thinking of her, completely wrapped in white linen, dancing away from him and Calliope. And when he played his music, he hoped she would sense it in the darkness and find stars.

Now Calliope had gone to find her. Rafe imagined Calliope with her moon face and long hair loosened from its braids, guiding herself into a blind darkness, tracing the sides of the narrow tunnel with the tips of her musical fingers. She would probably sing one of Ecstasia's songs to herself, he thought— Paul's lyrics like a lantern. Maybe her visions would lead her to Estrella. But what else was down there, in that place? The more Rafe tried not to think of it, the more horses and serpents and broken ravens with human heads reared and writhed and scavenged in a world beneath him, wild dogs bit the insect-buzzing dark, bloodless phantoms held their instruments, like shadows of the band who played above them in Elysia. What could Calliope see as she wandered down, calling her mother's name?

As if the tunnel were a huge drum he was about to play, Rafe lunged forward and was swallowed up.

He did not remember the tunnel. When he emerged, he felt as if he had been asleep for a long time. There was a metallic taste in his mouth, a silty tang of iron.

It was still very dark but, slowly, he was able to see. He was standing at some kind of a bank or shore. A cluster of figures waited, black water streaming at their feet.

The boat glided toward them and stopped. One by one the figures stepped off a narrow landing, their arms spread for balance, fingers grasping at the air. When they had settled in the boat, they held their arms close to their sides, rested their hands in their laps, and lowered their heads. Rafe joined them. They were wrapped in yards of white linen so that only their eyes were visible. The old ones. The boat moved through the water.

The only sound had been that foul-smelling water lapping, whispering, but as they neared another shore where some ancient subway cars stood decaying, Rafe heard something else. A pack of dogs rushed howling down the bank, their bones sticking out under raw flesh and patches of fur. They waited at the edge of the water, baring their teeth so their gums seemed to buckle.

The cloaked boat man took something that looked like a long, hollow bone and pressed it to his lips. As he blew strange notes through the shaft of the instrument, the dogs began to shiver and whine, then skulked away into the darkness. Rafe massaged the skin of the small drum he wore like a weapon. He followed the others out of the boat.

Calliope, he thought. And then he said her name aloud to make sure he still knew how to speak.

The cobblestone streets of Under wound like those of Elysia, but here there were no candy-colored lights, no people dressed as angels, as cocktails, Egyptian wall paintings, cowboys, Indians, or dolls. Here, the buildings did not offer promises of their warmth through windows full of glowing gold light, laughter, music. The buildings were blank, windowless, impenetrable. The only light came from a row of gray street lamps. Rafe stood alone at the end of an alley. The other passengers had vanished.

That was when he saw the dogs again. Their yellow eyes flashed and their jowls quivered as they scrambled forward. And Rafe remembered the boat man's bone flute. His hands fell upon the drum slung over his shoulder.

It was a stark rhythm Rafe played, echoing against the buildings as it tried to escape the confines of that city beneath the earth. He leaned back, sucked in his lips and cheeks, and shut his eyes to the approaching pack of fur and teeth. His palms showered down again and again, flat and callused on the skin of the drum. His whole body responded to each beat, but he did not turn and run—stood half-waiting for the ripping and snarling animals.

Instead, there was a whimpering, a pained whine and scuffling at his feet. The dogs cowered there, some flattened against the stones with their paws pressing on their skulls. A few still bared their teeth, but most looked toothless, beaten, broken by the music that came from that drum, those hands. When Rafe started to walk through the streets, they dragged themselves after him.

The streets continued to wind, buildings looming above so that he felt he was moving through a series of tunnels. A few old ones in white drifted past. When they saw the dogs, they vanished back into the buildings. Some noticed the low-slung heads and hunched spines of the silent animals and stopped, staring at Rafe with their nocturnal eyes. Looking back, he saw a few of them following behind him and the dogs, floating on the sound waves of the drum, remembering.

Rafe's palms were sore and his shoulders ached. Even as he moved forward, everything around him looked exactly the same.

Until he saw the first real color down here—the painful red neon of the letters. "UNDER," buzzed the sign. The dogs groveled in the dirt beneath it, then limped away. Rafe's burning hands collapsed at his sides. The old ones had disappeared with the last fading notes of his drum.

He turned to the door beneath UNDER.

When she had finished her act, balancing on the tightrope under the luminous flowers on her parasol, Lily wrapped herself in a cape and ran out of the tent into the streets. She ran on legs that seemed too fragile, past the bars and nightclubs and carnival grounds. Some people dressed in frilled baby costumes drank alcohol from nippled bottles. They stood under the street lamp that shone on ice-covered cobbled stones, so that the street seemed paved in wet light.

Lily kept running until she reached a deserted section of Elysia. On a back street at the edge of the town was the entrance to the tunnel. There were no guards, no bars even, just this opening in the ground. The cold bit like serpents at her ankles.

As she had night after night since her parents went Under, Lily entered.

There she was safe. Time suspended. She was no longer above, lonely without them. She was not yet below holding them, held by them, knowing that soon they would be gone again.

She got off the boat and moved through the streets lined with rows and more rows of hidden, decaying sick-rooms where the old ones lay. Some were outside, moving like haunted bones through the streets, some pushing others in ancient wheeled chairs. Some lay huddled under coarse blankets in the gutters. Lily looked at them; she always made herself look at them. It had not changed the way she felt, this looking, had not numbed her, closed off the shaft of icy air she felt howling through her when she saw them. But she must look, always look. Maybe one day it would make her do something.

Now, tonight, she did nothing. As always. It was her parents she wanted.

UNDER, the sign read. An ash-boy, his flesh corroding, peeling off in gray pieces, stumbled out. Lily went inside.

The room was full of suffocating red smoke and stone creatures with huge genitals. The addicts huddled in booths facing two stages, and on one stage a band wearing masks pounded on their instruments. Polished faces, imitating the faces of Elysia, hid the ash-boy flesh. In the central booth sat a man. He was surrounded by three hungry-looking women with tattooed arms. They had an ageless appearance, these women; they might even have been beautiful if not for the soiled flesh beginning to peel in places, the violent, colorless glow of their eyes.

"Lily! We've been waiting!" The man's voice came from some hollow cavern. He gestured to the empty stage, and she knew what she would do for him again.

She danced for him again, as she had danced night after night since her parents died. There had been more flesh on her body; it was easier for her to understand why he desired this then. Now, she was almost as emaciated as the women, Chloe, Shana, Leila, who sat beside him. But he watched her, they all watched her, greedily, the darkness of the club pouring out of their eye sockets or pouring into them. Tunnels. Like the tunnel that brought her down here.

"Let's see some more! Don't be shy with your Doctor!" he called from the booth.

She was weak tonight, hardly able to move her torso and hips. She was cold tonight, and the thought of baring her breasts for them seemed even more impossible than before. But she would do it. She knew she would do it again.

Slowly she unbuttoned her blouse, letting the fabric fall away. Her breasts bare, small, terrified. But somehow they were someone else's breasts, terrified without her. She thought of her parents—her mother's fragrance, her father's hands.

"Can I have it?" she asked. She was finished, standing in front of Doctor's booth looking down into the eye-tunnels.

His voice was always almost sweet, gentle with her, but hollow. "Have it? Your dancing was so mesmerizing I almost forgot. What is it you come here for?"

Chloe spoke then. "She wants something for her pretty head!"

"She wants her Orpheus," said Shana.

"Orpheus? Refresh my memory."

"It's a drug," said Leila. "It brings back the dead."

"She wants her mama and papa," Shana hissed.

Leila was sucking on the ends of her ratted hair. "They're dead."

Doctor's lips slipped over rotting teeth. "Should I give Lily her Orpheus, ladies?" He looked at Chloe. "What do you think?"

"She didn't dance like she meant it," Chloe said. "Her flesh isn't as fresh. She looks old."

Lily looked down. She knew it had begun, the aging. Suddenly, one day, it would happen; people above would notice it.

"True. True." Doctor's tongue moistened his lips. "But she misses her mama and papa. They went Under so early in her life. I can't blame her." He reached under the table and brought out the small drum, the long spoon. "You can have a beat of Sweet-Boy tonight, Lily. But work on those moves."

The spoon burst through the skin of the drum, and Doctor filled it with the powder that was inside. Then he grabbed Lily's arm and pulled her toward him across the table. He shoved the spoon up her nostril. Their bodies convulsed together. Lily pulled away, covering her face with her hands, and ran out of the club.

The girl was all Rafe saw. She was dancing, moving as if there were no gravity, even down here in this place of weight and filth. She was hardly a body but a shimmer of light and air. Her breasts were bare, her hips undulating, but he did not see her as displayed, exposed flesh. She was wings, mist, clouds. What floated above, walked above. He had known her for moments in that other world which seemed a dream now. Lily.

Then he felt the chill. It quivered along the hairs on his arms, seeping into his skin, penetrated his organs and bones. It was an ice draught in his stomach, a frostbite in his marrow. He turned away from the girl and saw the faces gathered around him, looming out of a cold red, sulphurous smoke. Flakes of grayish flesh peeled from their foreheads, cheeks, chins, noses. They would peel away to bone. Desire for what was lost had burned their eye sockets deep into their heads.

This was another Under—the addicts' Under.

Rafe reeled in their midst, breathless, buried, looking for Lily. He remembered his drum and fell upon it with all the force that remained in his body. As the addicts backed away, mesmerized, Rafe stumbled towards the stage where Lily had been, but she was gone. And then, through the membrane of smoke, he saw her leaning over a table, a man's face hovering above her, disembodied, grinning. For a moment, Rafe had the sensation he was looking into a mirror. His own face felt frozen, contorted into that same ravenous grimace. He reached up to touch his mouth, his eyelids. And when he opened his eyes again, Lily was disappearing out the door, running, as if she were following something, someone, flinging herself into invisible arms.

He followed her.

Outside he could breathe better, away from the red smoke, but the air still had a density, a metallic taste. He turned in circles like a dog.

She was running still, or blowing, though there was no wind, and he chased after. He called her name, but as in a dream, his voice lodged in his throat, so he kept drumming. She stopped suddenly but did not turn. She did not seem to hear him, but her movements echoed what he played. Or perhaps he was echoing her.

The dance had taken over. It was a dance about longing. It was a dance about finding what you thought was lost forever. The tremulous, circular, panicked searching. The swooning, sinking ecstasy. Finally, the drugged peace. He watched her as the addicts in Under had watched him, half-blinded with tears. He imagined cascading willow trees, blossoms growing in the earth and air, green rain, perfect animals that were not half-human mutants or groveling mongrels. He imagined finding his mother, finding Calliope. Falling into their arms.

Then he saw that Lily was moving away again, but this time he was not quick enough. The sight of her had stunned him, and his drumming had drawn all the adrenaline into his arms and hands. His legs were weak. She was drifting into darkness. She was gone.

Rafe stood alone on the dark street, tasting his iron-flavored tears, half listening for the dogs and the addicts, trying to preserve Lily's dance in his mind. He knew he must find Calliope. He knew he must get back up.

LILY'S ORPHEUS SONG

My mouth puckers with the bittersweet. This is the taste of longing—like the pomegranate. A thin film of translucent sweet coating the tiny, hard, white cores.

Mama. Papa. You stand in the dark street with your arms open.

Every time it is the same. It is not just seeing you. It is touching you, being held by you after . . . No matter how many times the Orpheus brings you back to me, when you come again I am stunned with this—finding what seemed lost forever. Mama, your wrists beat with blood. You wear your circus skirt, the one you wore to walk above. It is covered with mirrors reflecting me. Papa, your hands are warm, you in your ringmaster's top hat. In your arms, I am again perfect. Beyond time. We have escaped.

Oh, my Sweet-Boy. Oh, my Orpheus. In the form of a powder from the belly of a drum. You are the Poet who can even return the dead to the living.

My father will protect me. My mother will soothe me. Until they are gone, until they vanish. Then I will dance again. Until I must stay Under forever.

Under where the ash-boys wander.

Once I had a dream
She woke me from my sleep
Taught me to believe
Now I've lost her in a nightmare
But I'm going to find her somewhere

Even if it takes me
Takes me down
Under underground

Rafe played the Ecstasia song, thinking of how Paul had first performed it for the rest of them, looking so ferocious and almost demonic as he sang, until it was over and he lowered his eyes, then turned to them shyly like a child wanting to be told he has done something well. They had all been speechless as usual. Paul's words, and even the lingering, ghostly melody backed by a sudden, erotic beat, were like a premonition. Rafe wondered how Paul always seemed to know. Calliope's visions were a part of her, but Paul knew things in a different way—they came through him in the music. If only Paul's songs could help Rafe now.

Rafe gazed up and down the street at the rows of windowless stone buildings. They offered him nothing, no clue to where he might begin to find his sister. But he kept playing.

He felt the cold, dry touch on his arm and turned to see an old one shivering beneath linen mummy-wraps. The small figure pawed at Rafe's arm with starched, wrapped fingers, beckoning, and he followed.

Because the buildings and streets were all almost identical, Rafe could not tell how far the old one had led him. He felt as if he had been walking in circles. Only an occasional figure in white, crouched in the gutter or hobbling over the cobblestones, gave him the sense that he was actually going somewhere. But finally the old one stopped and entered one of the structures. Following, Rafe saw the chill, gray sick-rooms he had heard rumors of, the rows and rows of sick-beds filled with wrapped, waiting old ones. He saw the plaster casts of each of them, made when they had first arrived, waiting at the foot of each bed. The casts were clean, white, unwrinkled, blind. They would hide the corpses when it was time, the way the linen wraps hid the aging bodies now, but more perfectly; the wraps were soiled and tattered and the eyes gazed out.

Rows and rows of beds, of old ones, of plaster figures. The echo of footsteps. Rafe did not play his drum now.

And then he recognized one of the plaster women. He knew that the flat white eyes were gazing upward, although there was no pupil. He knew that the hands could soothe the pain in your head or the burning of your flesh if they had been real. He recognized the smile that was there in spite of everything.

On the bed behind the plaster cast of his mother, Rafe saw Calliope's back, her braid of hair, as she sat bent over the figure in the bed. He moved nearer, and she reached out for him without looking, drawing him down beside her. Together they stared into the eyes of the woman in the bed, the woman who had once breathed beneath the plaster as the cast hardened and, before that, long ago, breathed beside them in the world above.

"I saw her before," Calliope whispered. "She saw me. She said I had flowers in my hair and wore sheaves of corn. She said my hair was water and the sun was in my face. She said there were stars falling from my eyes. 'You are a white horse,' she said, 'the color of the moon.'"

Then Calliope fell against her brother's chest, draping herself over the drum as if the air had been knocked from her. He stroked the top of her head.

"We heard you, Rafe. We heard you playing. Not just me. She heard you, too."

He allowed himself to look at his mother's lifeless body once more. She had seen her mirage again, in the face of her daughter. It glowed there still, within her pupils, fading as he watched.

A group of old ones had gathered at the foot of the bed. They were cracking the plaster cast into its two halves like some kind of great, fossilized cocoon.

"Come, Calliope," Rafe said. "We have to leave now."

She stood slowly, stiffly, like an old woman, and leaned on him as they began to move away.

"And not look back," she murmured.

At the loft, Paul and Dionisio were waiting. When he saw Calliope, Dionisio dropped the glass he was clutching, and it smashed on the floor. The shattered fragments seemed to blaze there as he ran and knelt before her, his arms around her hips.

"Are you all right? I'm sorry, baby-girl."

Wide-eyed and pale, she touched his black curls as if she had never felt anything so soft before.

Rafe saw Paul watching him from across the room. The gaze reminded him of something that had passed between them a long time ago, and he wanted to shade himself from it. But Paul had already looked away.

LOVE WINGS

I dream of a place
where wings fill the sky
we dance like an earthquake
drink ambrosia wine
you do not cough
my skin is at peace
the sky full of hawks
the pulse of the earth
like my hands holding you
pulses with the drum of horses

The water you ride
is an animal too
star foam mane and wings
it carries you
pyramid sparkled sands
a dazzle of hills
that pulse like your life in my hands
pulses with the drum of horses

Love Wings 2

"*I saw you,*" Rafe said.

He was standing below the rope gazing up at her. She turned her head, swaying precariously for a moment. When she regained her balance, she swung lightly off the rope to the floor, her slippered feet whispering on the mat. She stared at him.

"What?"

"I'm sorry. I wanted to tell you that I saw you there. Under. And you saved me in a way. I mean, you helped me find my sister. I know you don't know what I'm talking about—I called your name but you didn't hear. But it was like you led me to her." He stopped, breathless.

"What are you talking about? I'm trying to work. You can't just come in and . . ."

"I'm sorry. I know. I had to tell you. I couldn't believe you were down there. You were so beautiful. Just seeing you made me remember I had to get Calliope and come back up." He was speaking too quickly.

"I don't know what you're talking about. Please leave me alone."

"Lily, I saw you."

"I don't go there. I've never been. Please."

"All right. I won't ask you about it again. I just wanted to thank you."

She hesitated. "I thought you said you would never go."

"My sister, Calliope, she wanted to find our mother. She saw her for just a moment before . . . I found Calliope and brought her back. But that place . . . It feels like . . . I'm afraid to go to sleep now."

For the first time since he had spoken, Lily's eyes softened. When he moved towards her she did not flinch or back away.

"I want you to come see my band—the band I'm in. We're playing next festival night at Club Carousel." Rafe reached into the pocket of his jacket and pulled out a piece of paper. She hesitated. Then she looked into his eyes and took it.

"I hope you come."

She nodded almost imperceptibly and started to walk towards the curtain. Then she turned back. "Just forget about that place," she whispered.

On the carousel stage, among wild-eyed wooden horses baring their teeth, Rafe played drums with the band. He was deep in the current of the music, both its creator and what it created, the way he felt only in water, when he saw her standing, watching him. She wore a pink velvet hat shaped like a rose that hid most of her face, but he recognized her eyes and her body in the light dress—mostly her arms, so white they reflected the blue lights of Club Carousel.

When the last song was over, he went to her. He knew by her face that she was under the spell of the music, but unlike so many who heard Ecstasia, she was not seeking out Paul and his radiant, scarred voice. It was the beat beneath Paul's voice that had moved her.

"Come meet everyone," Rafe said.

Calliope, still paler and thinner than before she went Under, was leaning against Dionisio as he drank from a big bottle of raspberry liqueur, thick with fruit. Paul stood alone, deeply involved with the cigarette between his lips.

"That's Dionisio and my sister, Calliope," Rafe said. "This is Paul."

Lily smiled. "You're really wonderful."

Paul looked at her, then at Rafe, then back at Lily. Dry ice, Rafe thought. Ice on fire.

"It sounded beautiful." Her hands flickered as she spoke.

Paul blew some smoke, turned and walked over to Dionisio and Calliope.

"He gets like that. I'm sorry." Rafe wanted her eyes again. "What do you want to do? We could go eat or dance or get a drink. Dessert? Everything?"

She laughed.

Her arm felt almost breakable in his as they left the club.

⌒

The Toy Store Tavern was filled with huge china dolls and rocking horses; the waitress was a mechanical doll with veined glass eyes. Lily ordered angel hair pasta, summer squash soup, persimmon salad, strawberry shortcake, a champagne cocktail.

"You know how to order," he said. "Most girls I know seem scared of food."

"I can understand that. We've supposed to be thin, like kids."

He studied her, sitting there, as the doll brought her meal. In a way Lily resembled a child, but there was something else in her face. Something almost—ancient, Rafe thought. She was vibrant and also a wraith already—far away, air.

Later, when they danced at another club, she was all life. They spun sweating around the dance floor to the beat of the African drums. The other dancers moved back to give them room—these two in their vivid clothes, hypnotized by each other. Suddenly, he saw her slow down, bend over, her face in her hands. She was coughing.

"Lily, are you all right?"

"I'm fine. I'm all right. This smoke, though . . ."

He led her off the dance floor and touched her bare arm. The sweat shone on her collarbones, on the tiny bones at the top of her shoulders.

"Let's go to the ocean."

They drove north along the coast in the white, finned car that had belonged to Rafe's father. The sky was beginning to pale. Rafe drummed on the dashboard as he drove. They parked at the end of the deserted pier and began to walk along it over the poison-dark water. Around them, abandoned carnival booths and hot dog stands were falling into decay. No one came here anymore since the toxic spills. Once, not so long ago, it had been another color even this far south. Rafe remembered it— blues, greens, not like the electric blues and greens in Elysia. He had stood at the edge of the pier, staring down. His mother had called to him, "Look, Rafe!" The toy clowns in the carnival booths were exploding to fire. But he had wanted to stay where he was.

"Paul and I used to surf north of here where it's still clear enough."

"That's what I'd like to learn."

"I could teach you. With your balance . . ."

"My best wet dream is that I'm surfing and I master the most impossible wave knowing I will live forever," Paul had said once. Rafe remembered the song: *You are the ocean and you are the stream / you shine like water you are my wet dream.* He looked at the poison waves, at Lily, and wished he could take her somewhere clear, clearer even than where he had gone with Paul, an ocean of their tears or the morning flower moisture in the greenhouses.

They walked the pier, feeling the slightly oily spray on their faces, smelling the waste disguised with salt and wind.

Why are we here? he wondered. He thought of his mother's letter. The oasis she had dreamed of for him and Calliope. *A shimmer of green and the startling cool sheen of water. The water will shine over their bodies, will fill their mouths.* And his mother was gone.

Why are we here? But where do we go?

When Lily began to shiver, he put his jacket around her and they drove back to town.

It was still very early. Rafe followed Lily up some stairs to an apartment cluttered with things, a history of things. Some were what he would have expected—stuffed bears wearing tiny hats or wreaths of dried flowers, dolls with china teeth, glass eyes and braids of real hair, embroidered gloves, laces, petticoats, fan-shaped perfume flasks, jars of powders and creams. But there were other things—a wedding dress, all lace, pearls, and yellowing satin roses hung from the ceiling, its train pooling on the floor. And then there were the flowers—stiff, white lilies carefully arranged on a coffinlike dresser, the tiny, white skeletons hanging on threads, the old one's rocking chair. The walls were a collage of floating watercolor faces, origami birds, bows, postcards, and photographs. Most of the photos were of Lily as a child standing with a man and a woman in circus clothes.

Rafe touched the wedding dress delicately, half-expecting it to disintegrate in his hand like a cobweb. "It's like someone's whole life here," he said. "Someone who has . . . lived a long time above."

In Elysia, most homes told only of childhood and the short time just after. No weddings, no objects of age, no death.

"Well, part of it is a life," Lily said, picking up a china doll. She stroked the yellow braids. "And part of it is made up. I shouldn't get so attached to things, though."

"I don't know," Rafe said. "If you need them . . ."

She put down the doll and lifted a crystal ball to the light. "Yes. I really *need* this practical object to predict the future with."

"No, but it seems like they tie you to the ground a little or you'd float away."

She spun on her toes, still holding the crystal ball.

"What do you see in there?" he asked her. The ball glowed in her hand, reflecting the tiny skeletons, the flowers.

Lily stared into it for a moment, and again he saw the shadows overtaking her. She shook her head slightly, her hair floating out. "Sleep. I'm so tired."

Rafe wanted to touch her. But he was afraid. When he made love, there was always the overwhelming sense of fatigue, guilt, and worst of all, the loss. It left him awake with it, watching the girl beside him sleep. He could not go through that now. But he saw Lily, her eyes downcast, her chest quickening with breath, and he wanted to touch her.

"Lily . . ."

They were wrapped together, their mouths pressed, the delicacy of her bones speaking to him beneath such a thin layer of dress, of flesh.

Then they both pulled away; his hands dropped to his sides. It would not be now.

As he left her, the yearning in him was worse than any loss he could imagine. He wished he had not let go.

~~~

That morning, after Rafe left, Lily had the dream again. In the dream, a boy was sitting on a tiny island in the middle of an icy body of water. In the dream, Lily knelt at the shore that was lined with towering buildings shining gold in the darkness, the homes of giants. She was watching the boy. She was naked and bent over, her hands cupped to the water, but somehow she could not drink. Her throat was full of sand, her skin transparent like a snake's, and beneath it her tendons were empty riverbeds. She was a drought. The water evaporated in her hands or, when she put her mouth into the lake, on her lips. In the dream, her need for water and the boy were the same.

But when Lily woke up, she knew how he felt, she knew as she always knew after this dream. She knew the bones of his shoulders, back, wrists, hips. She knew the skin, smooth on the bones, how he smelled, how he tasted like the rainwater that filled flowers in another time. She could never reach him in the dream but she knew him. She had had this dream again and again ever since her parents had died.

Lily sat up. Why hadn't she realized before? This boy, dreaming on the island, this boy out of reach. She knew his face so well—the fine features, the cheekbones so exposed, the black hair and lashes. His body pure as the animals that were gone now. It was Rafe.

The room was already dimming with evening again, the green neon mermaid outside Lily's window flashing. She had slept all day; it was time to go Under. She looked at the picture beside her bed. Her mother. Her father.

I am dying for ghosts, Lily thought. But she was wrapping herself in her cloak, ready to go back down.

LILY'S ORPHEUS SONG

Why did you leave me? You never talked about it. I would rather have died with you in that car than this. All of us at once. Quickly. I don't want this. At least we could have all been to-gether in the car. But you never talked about it. You never even used the word dead.

I am wandering the streets in the rain. The puddles swirl with colors like the inside of abalone shells. The streets are empty. No children suckling on champagne. No cars. So few cars here. No one wants to go far. All the parties they could want are right down the street. But you had that car. I remem-ber you were always so proud of it—two-tone pink and black, sleek and bright, otherworldly.

One night you left Elysia for a drive. You never left your candy city. But that night you took the car and flew into the darkness. Wingless, you crashed among the rocks. Both of you at once. You couldn't have planned it better, more mercifully for yourselves. You never had to get old or go Under or lose each other. But me, you left me. You never told me about it. I was supposed to believe an accident. Why didn't you tell me?

So now you come back to me when the Poet calls you.

A car drives out of the mist, flashing its headlights. It stops in the street ahead. The back seat door swings open. And I hear my name.

I run toward the glossy pink-and-black car, the halo headlights. The joy is swelling up in me like a dream where you are both there, sitting on the end of my bed saying, "We were pretending. We never really left, Lily sweetness. It was only a dream." Then I wake up and you have crumbled to dust. But in this dream I will be able to smell the perfume and smoke drenching your hair and clothes and to feel your kisses. And when I wake from this Orpheus vision, I will know I can find you again and again.

When I get in the car, you look so beautiful in your circus makeup. Father, in your top hat and satin-trimmed tuxedo, your arm around Mother with her jewel-starred chignon.

"Darling, we are so sorry," Mother says.

She always says she is sorry. There are tears on her face, but they seem to have frozen there, gilding her cheek as if they are made of glass.

Why did you do it? I say. Tonight I have to ask them. Sometime I can forget.

"We were so afraid," my mother says. "We couldn't go below. We couldn't go into the desert. And we couldn't lose each other."

You lost me.

But no:

"We are all together now," my father says.

Do you know how I do this? I ask.

You exchange glances. You look back at me. How sad you look, pleading. You remind me of children cowering from punishment.

"We thought . . ." my mother says. "Are you hurting yourself, darling?"

I cannot tell her about the man. I cannot tell her what these moments of life have cost.

Can we drive? I say. Will you sing to me?

When I was little and I couldn't sleep, you took me on drives through the city. You would sing to me. I was warm under blankets, wrapped in my parents' song. I imagined the car as the song hardened into substance, a world of glass and chrome formed of music.

So easy to destroy that and what it contained. Why wasn't I with you when it happened? Curled in the back seat dreaming to your song.

This phantom car will not go off a cliff. But it will vanish, leaving me huddled on the street crying, waiting for the next time. Waiting for the gift that my dance will buy. For all of us.

⌒

"Rafe, you look tired," Calliope said when he returned to the loft.

He shrugged.

"You should get some sleep. Are you all right?" Calliope took the cake layers out of the oven and began to spread them with jam.

"Don't worry about me, Callie. I want you to take care of yourself after all that."

She ignored him. "You've got to slow down."

Dionisio was sitting at the drum table with Paul. "So how's your girlfriend, Rafe?" he called.

Rafe's fingers drummed on the counter.

"She's beautiful, don't you think, Paulo? Like Calliope's vision. But does she float?" Dionisio came into the kitchen with his bottle.

Paul followed him, smoking. "She doesn't look well. Is she an ash-girl or something?"

Rafe's nerves clashed like tiny cymbals. "She's just really fragile."

"Does she eat enough?" His sister was swirling the pale chocolate cream onto the cake. "You should bring her over here."

"Thanks, Callie. No, she eats."

Paul stared at him. Rafe knew what the tone of Paul's voice would be, even before he spoke.

"Rafe, you've got to commit a little more right now. You just didn't play well enough last night. Some people from The Apollonian are coming to hear us next week. Look at you, boy!"

"I've been working really hard." Rafe's sweat was cold and thick on his skin.

"I think you need to straighten out your priorities."

"Stop it, Paul," Calliope said. "He was on last night. We all were. And it's been a hard time lately."

Dionisio raised his eyebrows at Paul. "What's with you?"

"If we are ever going to do anything, we've got to work. You all get caught up in your little romances and you forget what we're supposed to be doing here. Ecstasia is for all of us. If you can't keep up—"

"Paul!" Rafe felt dizzy with fatigue. He wanted silence.

"Boys, boys," Dionisio said.

Rafe left the room.

The next day, Rafe went back to the circus tent. He stood watching Lily poised on the rope, her legs shining, her face almost ecstatic. She did not notice him until she was on the ground again, wiping the sweat from her temples. He touched her bare shoulder blade, and she turned.

"How are you?" He was whispering, not wanting to disturb the temple of stillness she had built around her.

"I'm fine. A little tired today, though." She slipped pink woolen leg warmers over her stockings. He noticed a strained look around her eyes, but she was smiling.

"I came to invite you to our loft next Festival night. Some people from The Apollonian want to hear us."

"I'd love to come," she said.

Just then, the Old Clown rode past. His hollow, sorrowful eyes were startling in his smiling face, or, Rafe realized, it was the smile that startled, the smile painted among the wrinkles. The clown stopped the unicycle and got off.

"Do you mind if I try that?" Rafe asked him.

The clown's voice was sandy. "Please do."

Rafe took the unicycle and lifted himself onto it, clenching

with his thighs, balancing with his arms, his spine straight as he
wheeled in circles around Lily. The clown's eyes seemed to fill
for a moment before he disappeared into the shadows.

"I didn't know you were a circus performer!" Lily said.

"My sister and I used to perform for my mother."

He remembered Estrella in her white fur, clapping her
hands. As she clapped, the light sparkled on her rings. He was
wearing one of her scarves wrapped like a sheik's veil, and doing handstands. Calliope was playing the flute, surrounded by
her stuffed lions and bears.

"What got you started?"

"My mother used to say, whenever we got upset she'd say,
'Rafe, you need to play your drums,' or, 'Calliope, dance.' It was
changing anything dark into something beautiful with your body."
He stopped, letting the unicycle slip to the side, his weight balanced on one leg. "But it's hard sometimes." He looked away,
squinting into the firmament of lights above them.

"You miss her," Lily said. In her voice, he recognized the
knowledge of loss.

"She had that sweetness, that sweetness, you know, some
people have. It's just there in them, and you know right away.
You have that."

Lily looked into his face as if she were dreaming.

"Come on my shoulders," he said.

"What?"

"Come on. You're light. Come on!"

He was wheeling around with her legs pressed on either side

of his face, her body balanced above. He felt tiny sparks whisking over his skin. The walls of the tent spun, sweat flew into the light. Their laughter circled them.

"Come with me. I'm so thirsty," she said when they had stopped. He let the bike drop to the ground and followed her.

Her dressing room was hung with veils, garlands, and leering masks. Candles burned, reflected in the large, oval mirror. Huge, pink balloons drifted, whispered across the floor. Lily poured two glasses of water from a carafe. The candle flames reflected in them. Rafe sat on the rose velvet chaise lounge watching her.

"I recognized you," she said. "I used to dream about you. I know how your body feels."

He took her small hand and pressed it to his face. "Do I feel like this?"

She put out her other hand, holding his face in her palms as if it were a delicate mask she was about to put on, Rafe thought. Then she leaned forward and again their lips were pressed so tightly, denying that they needed any breath to sustain them.

She was in his arms, her hair an electric veil across his eyes, when he pulled back. "Lily, I don't want it to hurt you. It seems like it could hurt you." Those breakable bones, those bruised eyes. He did not mention his own fears.

"No, I love you to hold me. I need you not to be afraid."

His heart was the blood drum he was always trying to find in his chest when he played music. Now, there was no mistaking it. He tried to keep the forceful beat, but too soon it was slowing, fading. In that moment, he knew that some time, finally, there would be no beat at all. Instead of turning away as he usually did after making love, he pressed Lily to him.

⌒

"I dream of a place/where wings fill the sky/we dance like an earthquake . . ."

Paul was singing, Ecstasia's loft was crowded with people in shiny costumes, feathers, peaked and veiled hats, matador hats and capes, beaded Egyptian headdresses. Among them was Lily. Rafe saw her there in front of him while he played. She was holding an armload of flowers and continually inhaling their scent with eyes closed, then raising her face to him. She looked as she had that night in her dressing room. He had not seen her for a few days; she had told him she was busy. Rehearsing and performing, she had said. But he had not forgotten the flower-drugged look on her face. Every night he had awakened with it in his mind and reached for her across sheets that were cool with her absence.

After the song, Rafe went to her. "I'm so glad you came."

She handed him the flowers, a bouquet almost too huge for her arms, lavish with pink stargazers and miniature electric lights. "I kept smelling the flowers while you were playing, and I smelled you, too. It mixed together. It was wonderful, the music. I mean, really. Wonder."

"You are, you're that." He didn't know what to say. "I'm sweating!"

"I'm jealous!" she said, laughing, wiping his brow with a handkerchief. "I'm not very good at being an audience."

Rafe set the flowers down, grabbed her hand, and they began to dance to the drums someone was playing. They danced wildly, finishing each other's movements, spinning like orbiting planets.

Finally, they collapsed together onto a pile of cushions. Paul walked by eating fluorescent candy.

"Paulo! I think they really liked us!"

Paul mumbled something and did not look at them. He kept walking.

"Is he all right?" Lily asked.

"He just gets like that. I'm sorry you have to see it."

"I don't mind for me, but it seems like it's hard for you."

"That's just Paul. He can be really harsh sometimes. Sometimes I wonder why I let him treat me that way. I guess he's almost like a father."

Lily studied his face. "Who was your father?"

"He went Under early." Rafe paused. "Anyway, I always needed someone."

"So you had Paul."

"He really pushes me. One time, I broke my arm. I didn't know what pain was until that. Like this whole creature. And when I was in bed, Paul came and brought me weights and my sticks, and he made me work that arm. It killed—I was crying like a baby and he just sat there really quiet and then he said, 'Do you ever want to be able to play again?' I said, 'All you care about is your band,' and he said, 'Don't think you are such a hot drummer that I couldn't get someone else.' But he made me keep going."

"He's powerful," Lily said.

"When I first saw him, I was hypnotized." Rafe remembered Paul's face flooded with light as he sat in the gilt chariot on the carousel, singing. The veins in Paul's throat. The voice in his throat. That night, Rafe had imagined Paul made of gold. "I just wanted to be able to play music with him."

"How did you start?"

"I learned all the songs. Calliope was playing with him then and she heard me playing their songs and she asked me when I learned and I said, just from listening; I got his voice into my head after seeing them just once." Paul, rolling his eyes up in his head as if he were discovering the songs there, Lily, coming to life as she walked the tightrope.

"I wish he liked me more," Lily said.

"No, it's not that. He's just possessive. It'll be fine." Rafe was not ready to tell her everything yet.

"Tell him not to worry. I don't want to take you away from anyone."

Rafe felt the drumming beginning in him again. "I do. Want to take you." He lifted her in his arms and carried her away from the crowd into his room.

The chamois-covered walls seemed to pulse as if Rafe and Lily were making love in an animal's stomach. A sacred animal. In the belly of the drum. Candlelight chased shadows of their lunging bodies onto the walls. Rafe imagined fires deep in a forest, dancers flinging themselves onto the flames as the drummer's hands spoke for his heart. When it was over, he lay as close to

Lily as he could. Looking up at the ceiling painted with constellations, he wanted to tell her everything, at least something.

And then he was speaking, safe in her arms, in the drumroom. "A few years ago, I met this boy. We were friends. Then once he got some Beauty and the Beast. He must have gone Under to get it. We injected it into our veins and I have never seen . . . He was glowing like his skin was see-through and there was a blue light inside of him. We were really high, so I guess that's part of it."

He recognized in Lily's eyes the same protective look she had given the Old Clown. There was no judgment. No fear.

"Not that much happened," he went on. "But I pretended nothing did. He tried to talk to me about it, but I couldn't. Does that make you sick?"

"You shouldn't worry."

"I've been worried for a long time. For not treating him fair, too. And maybe I came across that way for a man to . . ."

"You are radiant, Rafe."

He buried his face in her hair.

"People worry so much," she said. "Just enjoy your body. That you can love. And you're alive."

Suddenly, her body shook with a cough that came from deep inside of her. She got up from the bed, naked, jarred with more coughs as she stumbled to the bathroom. Rafe jumped up and followed. She tried to hold the door closed with one arm, but he forced himself in and stood behind her while she leaned over the sink, still coughing. He could see the bones in her back, her painfully vulnerable spine. He reached for his robe and put it lightly over her. Then he looked into the white basin. It was splattered with blood.

"Lily! What is it?" He felt as if he had done this. Before, he had not been able to control his body thrusting into her.

"No, no, I'm all right." Still coughing, she gestured for him to leave her, but he remained there, his hands barely resting on her shoulders. Each cough shook him as if his organs were being torn away inside.

After that, Lily seemed changed. While she slept that night, he examined her bloodless skin, her hands, her eyelids. Something was different. What . . . ? His mind would not allow it.

In the morning, she put on her electric-blue kid gloves and dark glasses and she left.

He knew he would not follow her.

That day, he rehearsed with Ecstasia. He wanted the music to flood his head so he did not have to think. But even there, in the one place he had always been safe, he could not escape. His hands shook, the drumsticks leaping from his fingers, and Paul shouted at him.

That night, he tried to sleep but kept seeing the sink drizzled with blood. He saw her eyes and her hands. Age, that is what had been different. Fine wrinkles webbing around her eyes, hands spotted, papery skin. He understood why he had not stopped her when she left.

He called her, letting the phone ring and ring. Finally, he fell asleep, the receiver by his ear.

In the morning, he went to the circus tent, expecting to pull back the flaps and see her tightrope walking, the same Lily he had first seen, the Lily whose scent still filled his sheets. But the rope was just a rope now, not a passage across stars, not a miraculous path. Rafe stood beneath it, blinking up into the clusters of lights. The Old Clown came and stood beside him.

"I'd try to find her if I were you," the clown said.

"What do you mean?" Rafe whirled around. "Where is she?"

"You look for her. Even if it takes you down."

"What do you mean?" Rafe was almost shouting.

The clown turned and began to walk away.

Rafe grabbed his shoulders, then let go. The old bones reminded him of the skeletons dangling in Lily's room—worse, the shoulder had felt like Lily's shoulder. He shuddered.

The clown turned. "She is a magic girl. You find her. Even if it takes you underground."

Rafe ran again, ran through the streets to the upstairs apartment. There was no answer when he pounded on Lily's door. He called her name. The knob felt loose, and he managed to pry the lock open with his pocketknife. Inside the apartment, clothes were scattered everywhere; the bed was unmade. The flowers were dead in their vases, petals curling up brown like discarded snake skins. Rafe walked back and forth, looking for something. He picked up a photograph that was propped on the night table beside the bed. In the picture, Lily looked so young, so peaceful between the man in the top hat and the woman in the dress of scarves. Both the man and the woman had one hand on Lily's shoulders. There was something disturbing about the photograph, Rafe thought. The flowers they wore, the look in their eyes. All three of them like lovers still in the blind dream of new love.

His blood thick with fatigue, Rafe sat down on the rumpled pink satin comforter. He could smell Lily's hair, her bare skin on the sheets. He lay down, losing himself in the pillow, in the dream of a girl walking on air.

Sometime later, he felt a soft stirring against his cheek, breathed something, something. Twilight, as he opened his eyes. The green neon mermaid flashing in on him. Lily.

"Lily! Where . . ."

She had been caressing his hair, his neck. When he spoke her name, she turned away, hiding her face in blue-gloved hands.

"What are you doing?" she said, startled.

"What are you doing? Where've you been? I've been out of my mind. What happened?"

"I need to talk to you."

"What?" he shouted. "Look at me!"

She would not let him see her face. She pulled the veil from her hat down, but even hidden beneath it, she would not turn to him.

"I've been Under, Rafe. I'm sick and I'm going to stay in the sick-rooms there."

"You can't go Under," he said. "You're too young. You're just a baby still. What are you talking about?"

She spoke softly as the shadows deepened around them. "I'm sick, that's why. I'm aging really fast. I have to go. Because I'm going to die, Rafe. But that's better. I hope it happens fast. Anything's better than having to stay down there."

He sat up, fully awake now. "What are you talking about? You can't be sick. You're too young. What are you talking about? I can't believe that. It's not fair."

"But I am. I know. I can't always believe it either. But I am, Rafe, and now I need to stay Under so no one sees me getting like this. It brings them down."

"What? What are you saying? I haven't gotten to know you yet. We have hardly done any of the things . . ." He felt as if he were moving in a dream, unable to go forward.

"I know. I should have told you. But I didn't want you to get scared. I needed the time with someone. I'm sorry, Rafe." She touched his arm with her gloved hand. The soft bunchiness of fine leather.

"Why didn't you say anything? I wanted you so much. I told you things. I talked about pain. What was I talking about? I didn't know about that. Why didn't you stop me?" He started to shake her—shake her so that the shock of the cough would wake them from this. What had she said? "You needed time with someone? What are you telling me? Time with me. I thought you needed to be with me."

"Rafe, I didn't know it would get like this. I don't know if we even really do love each other. What does that mean? But I've never loved being with anyone so much. I couldn't tell you. You would have been afraid of me."

"I do love you. I don't know about you but I do."

"You don't even know me. You said so yourself." Her fingers gripped his arm. "You'll be fine. I want you to be, Rafe."

"What are you talking about? Going Under? Why didn't you tell me before? I'm not letting you go back there."

She breathed in with effort, suffocating on all of this, Rafe thought. "I have to. If I stay up here, I'll make people think about death. Look at my hands!"

She removed one glove and he saw the skin withering at the knuckles, the shiny brown spots like an animal's camouflage. "Look at me!"

In the darkening room, she turned to him, lifting the starry lace veil to show him her face. The skin was loose under her eyes and at her throat; she was a shock of whiteness. He did not turn away but took her hands, looked deep into her pupils.

"I don't care. You make me think about life more than anyone. You aren't going to go down there. I'll take care of you here. You'll get better here. I'm not afraid the way you think I am."

"But there's nothing you can do. You've got to accept that you can't do anything about this," Lily said. "People die."

DOWNTOWN

I would find you dancing downtown
in your net and tinsel gown
find you in places
filled up with faces
shadowed with roses, crosses and lace

I would glove your shoulders
bones beneath your coat
smell the burning petals
bend my head against your throat
take you out for coffee
speak of the winged child
I have dreamed of seeing
dancing in your eyes
and the snake of being
with his scales and scars
and his body filled with
all the rivers, animals and stars

We would drink the coffee
swallow it all up
until night was gone
leaving bare white dawn
the bare white cup
somewhere in the dawn light
I would find your kiss
I would not awaken
shut the pages closed on this

Never shut the pages closed on this

Downtown 3

CALLIOPE'S VISION

I see that girl, that one Rafe knows. Lily. That's her name. Like the flower. And she's as white as that, as those thick, white flowers, the only flowers Mother hated. I asked Mother why once, and she said she had heard that in other places, once, those flowers were death. Calla lilies. Lily. She is wrapped up, tucked under sheets. It is hard to see because she and the sheets and walls are all one white. But I see her, I see her eyes like two dark stains. And all around her are old ones. The tubes in their mouths drip some liquid into them, but they are becoming bones, the flesh peeling off them in layers. I hear Rafe's voice. "Lily!" He is calling her. He is trying to get down to her, but he cannot breathe beneath the earth. Without her, he cannot breathe.

"What are you doing here?" Rafe asked

Calliope stood at Lily's door. Rafe recognized his own face watching him, panic of his own eyes, as if his sister knew.

"I had one of them, Rafe." She hated to use the word vision.

"Come in," he said. "She's sleeping."

Calliope entered the apartment. Her eyes rested on the girl who lay beneath the pink satin. Rafe had arranged flowers around her, flowers with loose, soft petals, none of the stiff flowers Lily had filled her vases with before. There was a carafe of water beside the photograph of Lily and her parents. The lace curtains were closed, and Calliope could not see Lily's face.

Rafe gestured for his sister to follow him into the kitchen.

"What is it? Why haven't you told me anything?" Calliope asked him. Her shoulders relaxed visibly as if she were relieved to be in the lit kitchen hung with garlands of dried herbs, away from the dim room where Lily slept.

"What did you see?"

"I saw her Under."

"Callie . . ."

From the other room, Lily's screams broke the heavy air. Rafe and Calliope ran to her. She was sitting straight up in bed, her face in her hands, her hair tangled.

"Mama! Papa! Why are you looking at me that way? Why do you weep blood? Withered and pale like the ash-boys."

Rafe took her in his arms, gathered her small body to him. "Lily! Lily!"

She looked up, staring ahead of her, exposing a face age-raved, still eerily beautiful.

"Mama! Papa! I am descending. I need my Orpheus."

"Lily, what is it?" Rafe shouted.

"I need my Orpheus. I need my beat. I'm descending. Go down. Go down. Find Doctor. Get me my Orpheus. I will bury. Without my Sweet-Boy."

Rafe looked back and forth from Lily to Calliope. "What are you talking about? What is she saying?"

"Go down. Take the tunnel. Turn east of Red River. Turn south on Gorer. The club called Under. Doctor Death. Ask for Doctor. Say it's for me. I need my Orpheus. Say, 'just one more time.'"

"Calliope," Rafe said. "What is she saying?" He was kneeling by the bed now, his hands on Lily's hips, his hair falling into his face as he looked at her, then at his sister and back.

Calliope stood, watching. The calm had come to her face again, a calm that did not soothe, though; this was the masklike peace of her visions. "She needs that drug. It brings back the dead. She's an addict, Rafe. That's what's aging her. She's descending. Her head is full of the pictures. She wants you to get her a beat." It was not Calliope's voice, but the vision-voice, cool as porcelain. Rafe thought of the sink, spattered with blood.

"Lily! Tell me again!"

Calliope seemed to startle out of the vision. "No, Rafe. It's dangerous. You can't go."

"Mama. Papa. You turn to white dust. A powder of bones and teeth. Are teeth bones?"

"Tell me again," Rafe said. "The tunnel . . ." He began to re-peat the directions and Lily finished them for him, digging her nails into his arm.

He stood up. "Callie, wait here with her."

"You can't go again." Calliope tried to stop him, but he was already out the door.

⌒

In the club called Under, the ash-addicts with their shredding faces, glowing, colorless eyes sat in booths near a stage. Three women dressed in ancient, torn animal skins beat on their instruments, rolled their eyes and tongues. Rafe stood watching through the vapors of reddish smoke. The air smelled like damp soil in his nostrils.

When the women were finished, they went and sat beside a man in a booth. His eyes looked like earth-filled sockets in his bony face. He caressed the women's tangled hair and the backs of their necks with long fingers. It was those fingers mostly, wormlike in the tangled hair and knuckle-white all over, that made Rafe approach the man, thinking of what Lily had said, remembering. Doctor Death.

"Where is Doctor?"

The man looked up, his narrow lips spreading over rotten teeth. The gargoyles on the wall behind him watched Rafe with bulging stone eyes. "What can he do for you?"

"I have to ask him something."

"Why don't you sit down right here?" The man gestured with his fingers, but Rafe didn't move.

"You shouldn't be down here. Why would someone as young and pretty as you come all the way down? You've got it all up there."

"Could you tell me where Doctor is?"

The man bit his lip and drew in his breath. "He'll tell you the same thing, Old-Boy," he sighed. "He'll say, 'What is a pretty boy like you doing down?'"

"I need something."

The women on either side of the man laughed softly. Their eyes glowed in their heads.

"You need something? From Doctor? What could you need? You've got everything up there. Toys, food, music, beautiful boys and girls. What else could you want?"

The man paused for a moment, interlacing his fingers. Then he continued. "Not . . . something for your *head*? Beauty and the Beast? Candy Animal? Tattoo Orgasm? Venus Trap?"

"I need some Orpheus."

The women laughed again. The man smiled. "Some Poet, some Sweet-Boy, some Orph, some Eurydice-Seeker, some Orpheus." The smile was gone. "Why?"

Rafe thought of Lily sitting up in bed. He couldn't wait. "It's for Lily. She told me to ask for Doctor. She said it will be the last time."

At the mention of Lily's name, the women's faces became rigid. They turned to watch the man, and for a moment he hesitated. "Oh, for Lily. Now why didn't you say! Lily needs her beat!"

"She's coming down too fast."

"Little Lily? How sad." The man's voice was oozing. "She need to see her mama and her papa again? I'll help you out, Old. You just send Lily down here for a little dance. She'll get her beat."

"She can't come. She can hardly move."

"But she must. That's the bargain. A beat of Orph for a dance."

"You have to help her!"

"I'm sorry. A beat for a dance. A dance for a beat."

Rafe leaned nearer, seeing Lily's face in his mind, the pinched expression as she lay beneath her sheets. He leaned nearer still, despite the rotten smell, the peeling flesh. "Please!"

The man opened his mouth, a dark cavern; for a moment it seemed filled with soil. "Ladies, show him the way out."

The women stood, and Rafe felt their fingers wrapping around his arms, their hair suffocating him as if he had swallowed clouds of dust; he smelled the decaying sweet stench of leaves and dying creatures. He could hardly struggle. Although their tattoo-scarred arms were thin bone, they were powerful.

Rafe lay in the street outside the club. Finally, he stood up, muscles shaking, and tried the door. It would not open. Like someone who has dreamed of being buried alive, he started back to Elysia.

Rafe opened the door of Lily's apartment. The room felt airless. He saw Calliope kneeling by the bed. She turned to him. The wet in her eyes shone in the lamplight. When he came closer he saw his sister's fingers on Lily's wrist, saw Lily's changed face, Lily looking as if she had been bitten, he could only think, I have forgotten how to breathe. How did I ever breathe before?

He felt like a child waking in the middle of the night, feverish, nostrils hardened, who thinks, how do I breathe. Why didn't I think about it before? Now I will never think of anything else.

"We'll go to the coast," Calliope whispered.

They got out of the car and walked down the pier over the oily water, Calliope and Dionisio on either side of Rafe, Paul lingering behind. Rafe clutched his stomach, sickened with the sight of bubbling dark tides.

> *I would find you dancing downtown*
> *in your net and tinsel gown*
> *find you in places*
> *filled up with faces*
> *shadowed with roses, crosses and lace*

Calliope sang the words, her soft voice fighting with the sound of the waves, and Paul and Dionisio played their acoustic guitars. Rafe could not play, his body limp and deaf with grief. But he lifted the urn—it was so light how could it be so light even his weak arms could manage it—and tipped it, letting the ashes drift into the water.

> *I would glove your shoulders*
> *bones beneath your coat*
> *smell the burning petals*
> *bend my head against your throat*

This could not be Lily, Rafe thought, watching the ashes swirling, then swallowed. And where was Lily?

⌒

He wandered for days, back and forth, past the Toy Store Tavern where couples sat eating cake, drinking champagne, pouring champagne on their cake. He stood out in the dark street watching them lit up gold as if imprisoned in glowing champagne glasses in a dark bar.

He passed the circus tent. It looked deflated. He did not go nearer but stood watching, heard the jangle of circus music. Maybe she was there, in there, balanced on the tightrope, blindingly bright, her smile floating above him. All he could see in his mind was her smile floating, but he could not bring himself to go closer.

He woke in the night, crying out. But there were no nightmares, no images in his head. He wished for them—a picture of her, something in his mind instead of the emptiness. Even a horrifying image. Even a nightmare.

Orpheus, Rafe thought. He remembered Calliope's voice. "She's an addict. It brings back the dead."

Brings back the dead, Rafe thought, feeling the pocket watch his mother had given him ticking against his chest.

⌒

"Doctor, look who's here," said one of the three women at the booth, her bare breast exposed beneath a torn animal skin, her teeth like a gargoyle's.

So you are Doctor, Rafe thought as he stood in front of the

booth in the smoke-filled club. Doctor drummed his wormy fingers on the table.

"Did you bring Lily?" he asked, licking his lips. "A beat for a dance. A dance for a beat."

"Lily is dead."

"Dead? Do you hear, ladies? Dead?"

"I've come to get some Orpheus."

Again, the three women laughed at this, hiding their faces in their hair almost coyly.

"I understand. Lily is dead. You want to see her again," said Doctor. He paused. "This Orpheus is precious. Doctor doesn't sell it to just anyone. Especially some sweet, pretty boy from above. It is a complicated thing, this Orph. It only works a certain way. You have to need it. I need to see you need it."

Rafe shut his eyes, trying to see Lily's face. He could see nothing. Need. "Believe me . . ." he murmured.

"I'm sure I'll believe you. After you show me. What can you do that would entertain us?"

"I'm in a band."

"A band. What do you play?"

"Drums."

Doctor's eyebrows lifted. His laugh was like crumbling earth in his throat. "Drums? A beat for a beat! Let's see how high you play. You'll play with these ladies here, and if you're up-there, if you make me believe you need my Orpheus, then you can keep playing here. You'll get as much as you need. But you've got to show how bad you need to see her again."

He turned to the woman at his left. "Chloe, show him his drums." Then he looked at Rafe. "You'll play, they'll follow. They're experts at *following*!" He laughed again. "Just hope they don't follow you anywhere else."

The women surrounded Rafe, leading him to the stage. He felt their fingers bruising his flesh. There was a hush as the ash-addicts in the booths watched him. Rafe saw all the torn faces through the smoke, saw the eyes. He sat behind the drums, trying to imagine Lily here, Lily dancing for these people, for that man. He couldn't see her face in his mind. Down here, and without Ecstasia to hide behind, he felt stripped, as if the ash-addicts could see him naked, pale, see his chest with nipples erect and sore, his stomach, his hips, his groin, his thighs, everything exposed. He began to play. Paul was not here to hide behind, there was no voice but his own—rough, untrained, full with tears he had not cried yet.

> *I would find you dancing downtown*
> *in your net and tinsel gown*
> *find you in places*
> *filled up with faces*
> *shadowed with roses, crosses and lace*

The women followed on crude instruments, dancing wildly, rolling their eyeballs and their tongues. But Rafe was far away from them.

> *somewhere in the dawn light*
> *I would find your kiss*

I would not awaken
shut the pages closed on this

Never shut the pages closed on this

A figure whirled in his mind, the silvery fabric of her skirt catching the light.

When it was over, he found himself standing in front of Doctor's booth, looking into the dark spaces where eyes should have been. The women were standing on either side of Rafe, hissing and whispering, moving their hips, touching their breasts.

"You must have really liked her," Doctor said. "I saw her dance and I don't blame you. Fresh-flesh. Before she got greedy for her beats. You're heated, aren't you, Old-Boy? You need your Sweet-Boy pretty bad. Even after you saw what he can do. You played with some heat. I might just have to give you a little Sweet Orpheus. But not too much. I wouldn't want to hook you too hard. And age that fresh-flesh. Just a little beat to give her back to you for an hour or so."

He reached under the table and brought out a toy drum. "Make use of the time," he said, licking his lips.

Rafe started to take the drum. Sweat had soaked him——his hair, his shirt were wet through. He was trying to breathe.

"No, no, not yet. Don't be so impatient. Let me show you how this is done. Shana."

One of the women went to Doctor. He took a long spoon, forced it through the skin of the drum and filled it with a dark, pollenlike powder. Then he lodged the spoon in her nostril. At the same moment, both their bodies became rigid, then they opened their mouths and slumped down. Rafe looked at the woman's face. She had become ancient, a hag, her face creviced, dry as dust. Maybe he had imagined it, though, because as she staggered away, he saw that she looked as she had before. He wanted to turn and run.

"Shana's visiting her boyfriend," Doctor said. "Aren't you, Shana? She was pretty when she was up there. Until he died and she came hunting. These girls are tough ones—they're still alive after all the Poet."

Doctor's hands bit into Rafe's shoulder. Rafe fell forward over the table and felt the cold spoon jamming into his nostril, cutting the sensitive skin. He gagged, trying to breathe, felt his muscles and tendons wrenched from the bones.

"Lily!" he cried out.

The pain stopped, leaving his body feeling light, deeply healed.

"Rafe," he heard Lily say.

RAFE'S ORPHEUS SONG

"Rafe," you say. I hear your voice. It is your voice.

"Rafe."

I turn and see you there above, perfect on the rope. There must be a rope up there, but I can't see it through the smoke. It seems like you're walking on smoke.

You're more beautiful than I've ever seen you. Age hasn't

touched you. You're the girl in the photographs with your parents—your skin so clear and wet. The look on your face like a mirror of what is between them.

"Come with me," you say. You take my hand and I feel your palm and fingers. This isn't a dream. I feel your pulse in the hollow of your hand. I see only you—everything else fades in the red smoke. As we run. Up, up, up. I breathe, taking in clear, cold night as we emerge onto the streets of Elysia.

The circus tent billows and glows, but it's so late—when we go inside, the tent is empty. You face me, whispering my name. "Are you real?" I ask, and you don't answer. But I see you, breathe you, hear you. Here, in the lit tent under the rope you once walked, I'll taste you, feel you, here, in a circus tent—not the tent of my mind, a real place—we'll be a circus together. A lion in a hoop of fire, clowns, jugglers, stallions. We will be the acrobats entering each other in every position, suspended, contorted, transformed, reborn into a different creature. I stroke your head, your hair alive against my lips.

I had lost you forever and now I am holding you like a breath.

"Have you seen Rafe?" Calliope asked Dionisio.

"No, he hasn't been home. Paul's been out looking for him. You both worry too much." Dionisio offered her a sip of his bright green drink, but she shook her head.

"I don't know if he can handle this thing with Lily. I'm afraid he'll do something crazy. He doesn't understand about death," Calliope said. She went to the loft window and looked out at the winding street. It was a dark morning, the rain heavier than usual.

Dionisio laughed under his breath, rattling ice cubes in his glass. "Who does?"

"He doesn't believe that the closest he can get to her is by looking inside of him, in his music," Calliope said. "So he'll look everywhere else. I'm afraid of where he'll look."

"He may need to look everywhere first, take it to the edge and Under. The dark's good sometimes." Dionisio pushed his fingers through his black curls. "He's testing himself."

"I think Paul can help him. He looks up to Paul so much. But I never see Paul lately. Lily . . . it's messing Paul up too, almost as much as Rafe, and I didn't think Paul even cared much about her."

"He cares about Rafe too much sometimes, I think."

"Maybe he'll find him. I need to know where he is, Dionisio."

Rafe came into the room.

Calliope saw how her brother's white skin stretched over his cheekbones. "Where've you been? Are you all right?"

"I'm fine. I'm a lot better." He turned away.

"You don't look a lot better, boy. You look like you've been Under," Dionisio said.

"Rafe, I've been really worried," said Calliope. "You should let us know."

"I've been busy."

Dionisio spit a cube of ice back into the glass. "You've been down, boy, too far down."

"What are you talking about? Where's Paul?"

"He's looking for you." Calliope went to Rafe, reaching to touch his shoulders, but he pulled away.

"We know it's been hard for you," she said, and Rafe's eyes flashed from the shadows pooling in the bony area around them.

She left the room.

"Boy, I know. I see it in your eyes. I know about people who tried it to bring someone back. But it buried all of them. Stick to the lighter stuff. Try to forget, not remember. It's too expensive."

"You don't know."

"I know. It's sweet, that Poet, but it ruins you. Costs too much to remember. Your sister would lose her mind if she knew you were taking that. It'll hook you up, and you'll be down before you know."

"Rafe! I've been everywhere! Where've you been?"

Rafe turned to the tall blond man at the door and, behind Rafe's back, Dionisio caught Paul's eye and pointed down.

"I thought you weren't ever going to go Under again," Paul said. The scars showed up more on his cheeks; he hadn't slept all night, searching. "You're looking for her. She's not there, Rafe. She's dead. You've got to let go of it."

Rafe stood staring at Paul. He had no thoughts. Sleep. He left the room.

"He's had Orpheus. At least a beat," Dionisio said.

"I thought so. How did he get it? He isn't strong enough to handle it. Does Calliope know?"

"I don't think she knows for sure. But she's scared."

"We'll have to do something," Paul said. "He'll take it till he turns to an ash-boy."

RAFE'S DESCENT

I go back down to find the Sweet-Boy that will bring you to me. But Doctor says I don't play high enough tonight. He says to come back. But I'm descending! He says, "Down Down Downtown. Down Down Underground. A beat for a beat. See your baby with a beat." He laughs. His teeth are rotten. Sitting in that booth, never standing. Does he have legs? Or just bone stumps? I say, "I'm descending!" and he laughs. A rotting laugh.

I go out into the streets of Under. Descending.

What is that? Over there? A man is attached to a huge, revolving wheel. Hands and feet nailed to the rim. Body stretched just before the point of ripping. Ribcage and hipbones ready to burst through the skin. I don't stop to help him. A man, an emaciated bone phantom, dried saliva caked on his chin, reaches for a ripe, splitting fruit that hangs forever out of reach. Women lie in the gutter, howling, furious, trying to rinse the blood from their hands. I don't stop. There? A man is rolling a huge stone up a ramp and it continues to roll back down. His face is a cracked stone, his muscles shuddering. I don't stop to help. I cross the red river. On the bank lies a man screaming while a giant bird tears at the delicate tissues, the exposed mass of his liver. His blood pours into the water.

Why didn't I see all this before? Why can't I stop to do something? Looking for the entrance up, I hear your voice. I turn and see you, your dress billowing out like the circus tent. You open your mouth and there's a red light shining in you, shining out of your mouth, making your teeth glow red, as if they're glass. There's the entrance to the tunnel. You turn and enter. I hear the echo of your laughter and see the ghost of your dress. I follow you. In the tunnel I smell death. But I see you ahead of me, leading me back up away from the tortured ones—the wheels and howls and stones and blood.

We emerge onto the streets of Elysia and it's dawn. I hear your laughter—yours but it isn't yours; it's still the laughter of the tunnel, an echo. I turn and see you across the street. You hide behind a street lamp. I run to it, but you aren't there. Why are you running from me? Who are you? From the corner of my eye, I see the glow of your dress as you run down the alley. I follow you, thinking I will be like the man with the rock, the man being eaten by the bird, chasing you forever, never reaching you. But I'm running fast, faster than I would have thought possible. Orpheus. Sweet-Boy. Lily. I reach out, grasp your shoulder the way Doctor held mine that time before he filled me with the powder. Laughter like gravel. You spin, your hair wild, a tangle. Lily! But it is not you. The face I see is some other face, peeling, ashen, teeth bared, eyes glowing. One of them. She will eat my lungs.

When Rafe woke, he thought at first he was still Under. It was so dark. But then he threw back the cover, and the lights from outside his window flashed across his face. He took a deep, painful breath, the image of the Lily-creature still in his mind.

I lost you once. I can't do this again, Rafe thought, getting out of bed. He stood naked, shivering, one foot overlapping the other on the cold floor. His muscles ached and all his insides. He knew he would go back down.

The streets of Under were not full of bleeding men, broken men with stones and wheels, only the old ones wandering or slumped in the gutter. But maybe, Rafe thought, this wandering is the same torture. It must feel like forever, back and forth in the darkness—as terrifying for the old ones as the eternal pains his descent-visions suffered.

When the song was over, the women tried to caress him, their fingers bruising, tongues wagging, but Doctor told them to leave him alone. "You must have been up all night practicing!" he said. "You played much better tonight. I'll just have to give you your beat, Old."

RAFE'S ORPHEUS SONG

I drive to the ocean, far north up the coast. There are no evil pictures. You aren't with me yet, but I know you'll be with me. The Poet is inside of me. He'll give you to me.

I park and run down the steep path to the sand. It's cold, a cold wind, and no one's here. No one's ever here. The water's dark. I remember surfing with Paulo.

"My best wet dream," Paulo said. "Live forever." Live forever. Back from the dead. I look out at the water.

A wave breaks and I imagine riding that wave, the way my body would twist at the waist, the exact stance I'd need to master it.

And now, you burst out of the wave. I see your thin, white arms and your hair, black with water, showing the shape of your skull. You're walking towards me, slowly, slowly, each step a struggle as the water tries to reclaim you. But you're coming to me, your naked body gleaming with water, drops skidding down your white skin, pearling on your hair. I can almost feel you before I have you in my arms. Why are you pulling away?

"No, this isn't me. You're dreaming me. I'm just what you see in your head. I'm from the Orpheus."

But I can touch you and smell you. I tasted you. You taste like you. After we made love in the tent, I smelled the smell of our love on my body.

"I know. It's the Orpheus, Rafe. It's going to kill you. You can't keep taking it. You'll be his instrument. He's beating you like a drum. You're becoming hollow, but soon you won't even make any music. You have to stop."

I can't stop. I can't give you up again.

"You're alive. You've got to see that and live. What are you wasting time for? It's so short. You're destroying yourself trying to keep me. I'm dead. I tried to do the same thing with my parents. It killed me."

You're in my arms. I feel you. You feel like yourself.

"No. I don't feel like myself. I'm gone. Let go of me. Stop taking that death."

I'm afraid.

"I know. But you're strong. You can play like nobody, that's how you got it in the first place—you have that power over him. Your music. He needs you. So use it. Fight him with it. Fight wanting me with it. How do you think I died anyway? It was from taking the Orpheus to get my parents back."

Don't you want to stay with me? Lily.

You cover your mouth with your hands. Only your eyes, pupils beating like hearts.

What do you feel?

"I feel what you feel. Everything you feel. You bring me back. But I can't. I can't."

You wrench away. I feel the bone in the socket. You're running away from me up the cliff path to the highway. I follow you. At the top of the cliff, I stand looking up and down the highway for a sign of your dancing body, but there is nothing for as far as I can see.

BACK UP

I want to be with you
Over the Under
Under is stirring
Voices in darkness
Bones in the darkness
Follow us everywhere
Visions are blurring
Follow you anywhere
I'll lead you back from there

Back up back up
To where you came
Back up back up
All I have to do is sing your name

I want to be with you
Illness beneath us
Not hear the stirring
Chill in the darkness
Voices in darkness
Not hear them cry for air
Visions are blurring
Follow you anywhere
I'll lead you back from there

Back up back up
To where you came
Back up back up
All I thought I had to do was sing your name

Back up back up
And we'll remain
Unharmed, untouched
Immune from pain
All I thought I had to do was sing your name

Back Up 4

The first time Paul had seen Rafe playing the drums, had seen Rafe tossing his black hair as he played, seen the music filling the veins in Rafe's arms and hands before it came out through the drums, Paul had decided to go Under. He had heard of a drug called Beauty and the Beast, and he knew that was the only way anything would happen between him and this boy.

One evening, after Paul and Rafe had been surfing, they came back to the loft shivering, tasting of salt. Calliope and Dionisio weren't there.

"I have something," Paul said.

He remembered the way the drug had lit them up as if they had swallowed the reflection of twilight on the ocean. He reached out and cupped Rafe's glowing blue face in his hands, feeling the shape of Rafe's jaw, seeing those eyes looking up at him.

But it had been a mistake, Paul realized. After touching Rafe's lit flesh that night, he had felt more like the beast in the tale, had wanted to hide his face, his scars. Especially when, the next day, Rafe stared at him as if nothing had happened. They didn't mention it again, and Paul thought he would never go back down.

He wanted to forget the face of the man, the teeth, the voice. "Beauty and the Beast? Why would you want that? Beast, who is your Beauty?"

He would never go back down, he told himself. But now, Paul was going Under again. Not for drugs this time; he would not let Rafe turn to ash.

RAFE'S ORPHEUS SONG

I stand at the end of the pier where we scattered your ashes. The waves foam, churning. I want to leap into them, drown in that seething bitterness. Wind whips my hair across my eyes, lashing the eyeballs so I am half blind. I huddle into my jacket, shrunken and beaten. The Orpheus has not given me anything. I have come all this way and still there is nothing. The Poet is laughing to himself. His hair crisp and golden as Paul's and his eyes faceted like crystals; he is saying, what makes you think she will come back? His voice is the man's voice.

And then I am flooded inside with the liquid pounding. The waves unfurl, peeling back like when you pry open a bud, tight sheath after tight sheath and a bitter smell, the flower not yet ready, but there is something so perfect about it, there in your hand, revealed. Out of this wave-bud rises a bigger wave, and on that glides a surfboard color of pearl and a girl riding it. Her long, wet hair snakes over her body as she crouches to balance. Shell-encrusted seaweed woven in her hair like jewelled ribbons. Her skin is so white against the dark waves—it has a sheen, glossy as if the cold hasn't touched her, as if, naked as she is, she is clothed in glass. She looks up at me, the small face more pointed than I remember it, a little thinner, but it is your face.

Your eyes, salt-glazed, watch me from the shadows of their lashes as you crouch there beneath me. What is in those eyes? You are saying, no, you shouldn't have done it again, and you are saying, yes, look at what you have given me, breathed back into me, resurrecting me. An ocean, you have given me, and your face and your body. And then a wave comes up so I cannot see you.

I run down the pier hearing the boards creak beneath me; I am blind with wind, salt, tears. I throw myself off the side, not waiting for the steps, falling into the cold sand that cuts like fine glass. I run across the beach to the shore. Wanting, wanting. The Poet is shining. The Poet is smiling. He has forgiven me.

I know this because you are waiting.

I fall on my knees and the water beads down your hair and breasts, covering me with its sting. You close your eyes, touch your throat, cup your face in your hands. The glassiness is gone. You are not some chilly goddess I have dreamed. You are Lily. I see you shiver, I take off my jacket and put it around you as you kneel facing me. As I wrap you in it, I feel the ripples and pulses and swells and hollows of your body. My groin aches. You press your face against my neck, and although I cannot see or hear you say it, I feel the words, relief and fear.

"You have brought me back."

And you have brought me back.

We fall together into the cold sand, suddenly warm and fine as if it were the dust of sun-baked pearls and we, plunging into each other's forbidden, impossibly lost, impossibly found, bodies, bring each other back and back and back.

"What happened?" Dionisio asked Paul when he came back to the loft the next morning. Paul moved heavily, without his usual long-legged grace, as if weighted with the memory of the place he had been.

"I followed him Under."

"Where is he now?"

"In there, sleeping." Paul pointed to Rafe's door. "He couldn't get any so he came back here. I walked around alone for a while."

"Did he see you?" Dionisio asked.

Paul shook his head.

"What do we tell Callie?"

Paul collapsed on the cushions. "We should tell her. We'll need her."

"What can we do, boy? I've seen. No one can help unless Rafe wants it."

Paul thought of Rafe standing in front of the booth Under,

pleading. From the darkness where he hid, Paul hadn't been able to see Rafe's face, but he saw the plea in Rafe's back and shoulders. He saw the face of the man, as he shoved the spoon up Rafe's nostrils.

Rafe had run out of the club, gasping for breath.

"We can go down there and play," Paul said now.

"We play good but not that good," said Dionisio.

"Well, what, we let him kill himself?"

Calliope came into the room and Paul told her what he had seen, what he wanted them to do.

"It's dangerous, Paul."

Dionisio stood up and put his arms around her, more to comfort himself than for any other reason. The firm fullness of her soothed him. "Don't worry, baby-girl."

"Calliope, we have to go," Paul said.

"I'm going. We'll all go," Then her voice changed—the vision voice. "But we must stay clear. We must think of what we love and hold that within us the whole time."

Late that night, Paul went into Rafe's room. Rafe lay on the bed, clutching his stomach, thrusting his shoulders into the mattress. His hair was full of sand.

"Rafe, you have to stop," Paul said. His voice was scratchy and tender, his singing voice.

"Leave me alone."

"What do you want? Do you want to die? I can tell you some faster, easier ways."

Rafe gasped. "Leave!"

Paul came nearer. He wanted to place his hand on Rafe's stomach, help him relax the muscles, take in air.

"You were the one who didn't want to go Under ever. Look at you! Ash-boy addict. You are a musician! Rafe!"

"You just want me for your band."

"I want you to be alive. I know coming down feels like it will kill you. We'll help you."

"You just don't want me to get Lily back."

Paul hesitated. Was Rafe right? At first, maybe this was true. But now—seeing Rafe twisted on the bed and remembering him before, playing drums, running through the streets, poised on a wave—now Paul knew it was different.

If I could bring her back for you in a way that wouldn't hurt you. . . . You have always been the most alive person I know. I need to see that life or I'll go Under too, Paul thought. But he only touched Rafe's shoulder lightly and left the room.

"We must think of what we love and hold that within us," Calliope had said.

PAUL

Now I will go to find you.

When I first saw you, standing beside your sister at that Festival watching me sing, a wound opened. Scalding and blistering. I needed the cool fluid of healing cactus, the water, the secrets in your hands. You looked at me blindly. For years you walked beside me, spoke, played music, surfed with me, and you were blind.

Finally I found a way for you to touch me. Even if you didn't know what you were doing.

Now I will go to find you.

I thought I would never go down there again. After the last time. The first time. I staggered, then, into the dark, my head and hands heavy, thickening with each step. My teeth ached as if they were expanding in my gums. The hair stood up on my hands and the back of my neck as if I were growing fur. The scars on my cheeks were pitted, shadowy, as I went down.

"Beauty and the Beast? Why would you want Beauty and the Beast? Beast, who is your Beauty?" said the man.

All around me crouched statues of deformed little gargoyle men with long tongues and erections. I was choking. I would never sing again. Ash clogged my throat.

I would never touch you. I would stay here forever, kneeling before this man and his gargoyles. I would become a gargoyle, forever hard. I would burn and burn until I was charred ashes. And you were above playing your music. I tried to hear the drums in my chest. I remembered your face. Beauty, my Beauty.

That was what led me back up—holding the drug in my palm, the packet pressed against the life-line where it (the drug? my hand?) pulsed. When I found you, I was sure you could see the wound. But you only smiled, seeing nothing.

We drove to the coast. We were the only ones riding those waves. I could see you standing on the water, your shoulders poised, salt spray on your face. You were almost near enough to touch. But there was a whole ocean between us. You caught a wave, mounting, gliding, descending. Like a child you laughed, waving at me. Perfect, shiny, like a photograph.

Later we came back to the loft. You were wearing my jacket but you still shivered. Your eyelashes stuck together in thick star points. I wanted to see the pulse in your throat and wrists and chest. I wondered if I could see it. My own pulse must have been visible. I felt my whole rib cage beating from inside.

"I have something," I said.

You rolled up the sleeve of my coat and held out your marbley arm.

And Beauty and the Beast filled our veins until we glowed blue as our veins all over. Vessels of shining blue.

"You look like the ocean!" you said. "The sun and the ocean. I feel like I'm still swimming."

Then I think you saw the wound, but even that looked somehow beautiful.

It draws you to me. A tenderness fills you. You kneel down in front of me, tilting your face up. I take your glowing blue face in my palms. I wonder if my tears are as blue as yours. You place your open hands on my chest. Your lips taste of harsh, marvelous salt.

We slide down together. Our bodies are the waves. We roll and swell and crash blue salt foam. Your moist flesh, pressed against mine, makes me whole.

Only afterwards, when we woke from that azure dream and you realized what you had done, did I feel the tearing again. It was worse this time. A wound rubbed with salt. You weren't blind anymore; you still saw my wound, but now it sickened you.

Nothing has happened, your eyes said, as the ocean light drained from your beautiful face. *Nothing will happen again. I will never touch you again.*

Your face turned pale.

I became the Beast.

Now I will go down to find you.

Even if I must see the man.

DIONISIO

Calliope, Calliope. I need a drink now, baby-girl. But right, I know that's wrong. We're going to get Rafe. It's just that seeing all those ash faces . . . Once, I went down. I saw all those death faces, and I knew that that was me too in a way. Looking for something to make us forget. I didn't last long down below. The bottle felt safer. At least you don't have to face those sucking dealers. But it's really all the same. Maybe someday I won't want it anymore. You should be enough for me. Making me high with the shining flash of your body. That's what you told me to think about. What I love. You're always inside me like wine. What I love. Maybe we'll have kids someday, Calliope. Before we go below. I hope they have your wisdom, your shine. They'll be musicians, maybe. It won't be so hard to go below knowing they are above still. Sometimes I think it's harsh to do that to kids—bring them up in this play palace city on the edge of nothing. What do they have? Some pretty stuff for a while, some sweet stuff, some spirits in a bottle, and then the lifeless desert or the city-grave. But when I'm in your arms in our bed under the arbor, I understand why everyone keeps on going, keeps making more kids. Those moments of forever, of perfection, are enough. My kid will know this, we say, as we become our lover. Everything is worth this. At least if the lover is you, Calliope, then it's worth it. I'll go anywhere.

CALLIOPE

My three brothers, you are what I will think of as I return to the place below.

Dionisio, my soul's brother, I will say your name again and again and hold your hand as we move deep into the tunnel. I will imagine that we are in our purple bed where I taste your flesh, listen to the sound of your blood, feel the pulse of your dreams and the roots of your curls. All the pain in my bones dissolves. Our bodies become pools of nectar. If only this nectar was enough for you.

"Open me up," you say. "Help me to open." But it is you who open me, who have guided me into the mysteries—wild gardens, spilling, spouting fountains, cool violet light beneath the wisteria-draped arches, veiled women dancing, lynx cats striding, reclining men lifting flasks of nectar to their lips. All this is within the dream you give to me when our bodies join together.

I know you have sorrow, Dionisio. And that the ash-addicts we will see below will remind you of your need for something to ease it, to help you escape the thoughts of passing time. If only I could take away the bottle that stains your lips. You say I am your wine. Let me be your wine. As we go down, let me and your music be your wine. So that you and I can return together and open in the eternal garden of our bed. So that we can all return.

As the light fades in the tunnel, and the lights of Elysia become only a speck, the glimmer in a pupil, I will think of you, Paul. You, who are like a brother. I will think of you and your voice, and my mind will be flooded with light. I will remember how I came to play for you the first time. "Ecstasia," you said—the band you were forming—and I sweated and trembled as I stood before you. I felt sure I would fail. Your eyes were spotlights, floodlights on me. I never thought you would choose me that night. Your face was hard—all cheekbones—and your hair like pale rays. I finished and turned away, nauseous. I was almost at the door and you called me back. "Calliope," you said in that voice, the voice that haunts everyone who hears it, the voice I had dreamed of playing behind, beneath. I imagined my music spread like wings to carry that voice somehow, that treasure. "Where are you going?" you said. "Where did you learn to play like that?" "My mother," I said. "And then just working." "I went to the moon," you said. "It wasn't a barren desert. There were white flowers and silver water." You smiled at me. That smile will be with me in the tunnel, even if I lose sight of you. It will be my light.

And when we reach the river, I will think of my real brother, Rafe. As we step into the boat on the black water, I will think of the child-Rafe I cared for like a son although we are only a few years apart. And the grown Rafe, so quick and lovely and fragile even in your strength. You don't know what you are doing some days, spinning. You can't seem to ground yourself. You are storms, waves breaking, trying to fling yourself toward the stars while you forget the earth beneath you. You never had that earth, that solid place. Maybe that is why you sought the dunes that night. So tiny—you could have died there, trying to find the earth's pulse, the soft voice of a father. Your own father so cruel. Our father. And now you go back to the earth, beneath it, as if it will ease your grief, keep you from spinning into nothing, from crashing, drowning in your fierce waters. So you bury yourself. But we will find you and the river will carry us back, the boat will rock us like our mother's arms as we come back up.

You brought me back up once.

As Rafe played for Doctor that night, his stomach muscles tensed, pumping. He felt as if there was a battle going on inside of him, his body attacking itself. Before, the drumming had eased this, but now each beat drove the attack farther along.

After, he looked up from his drums. The second stage was illuminated, and through the red smoke he saw three figures poised like warriors. They all wore blank white masks, but Rafe recognized the way they stood and the instruments they held in their hands. At first, he thought they weren't real, but when he heard the music he knew they had come; they had come for him. As if in a trance, he left the first stage and went to join them.

> *I want to be with you*
> *Over the Under*
> *Under is stirring*
> *Voices in darkness*
> *Bones in the darkness*
> *Follow us everywhere*
> *Visions are blurring*
> *Follow you anywhere*
> *I'll lead you back from there*
>
> *Back up back up*
> *To where you came*
> *Back up back up*
> *All I have to do is sing your name*

As he played, Rafe felt something in his chest. A memory. A light. His chest expanded as if filling with light. Behind Ecstasia, wrapped in the glow of the music, he was safe.

"I'll lead you back from there," Paul sang.

They were a family now, or maybe they were one person. What was this spell that they cast with their music? Who was the singer, who the drummer, who played bass, keyboards? There was no separation. All together playing they became their own child. This child had heard melodies in the womb or, perhaps, remembered from another life. This child had a soul of fire and foam, wine and petals, amethyst, opals, ebony, and gold. It was not Paul or Calliope, Dionisio, or Rafe. An enchanted bower, a flooding fountain, a conflagration. This was the child they summoned. Ecstasia.

"All I have to do is sing your name."

But when the music was over, Rafe looked at Doctor in his booth. He thought of the Orpheus, of Lily. Just one more beat. There would be no more pain then.

He stood, rigid, trying to decide. But the decision was already made for him. Paul had Rafe's arm, the muscles weakened, watery from the drug, had it in his grasp. He was leading him out of the club.

Doctor and the women sat silently, cowering. The music had charged into, stunned them.

Voices in darkness / Bones in the darkness.

There was nothing they could do.

Finally, Doctor shifted his bones in the booth. He coughed, the thin layer of his flesh quivering. "The little drummer has some devoted friends."

Chloe gripped the edge of the table. "Especially the singer! I always *thought* he liked boys!"

"Poor little Lily! I wonder how she'd feel," Doctor said.

"I wonder if she at least got good penetration before she died," Shana spit.

"If he could get it into a girl at all," said Chloe.

"Now, ladies!"

Leila turned to him. "We know, Doctor. You liked Lily. She was a sweet thing. You liked to see her dance."

"You gave her her Orpheus pretty easy," Chloe said. "Just a few shakes of her little, tiny hips!"

"Jealousy?" Doctor said. "She needed to see her mama and papa. I was just being kind."

Chloe made a throaty sound. "You are so *kind*!" she said.

He moved his head slowly so that he faced her, his skull looming in the smoke-dark. "I wouldn't complain so much." There was no trace of the thin smile. "You keep getting fed. And if you're angry he doesn't want you, I'd consider the fact that you are so covered with scabs from all your injections that there is hardly a place on your body soft enough for a needle to penetrate."

"I'd like to penetrate him with a needle," Shana said.

"Well, he's gone now," said Leila. "We probably won't ever see him again. He's going to come clear."

Chloe's eyes glowed. "He won't; he's not strong enough. The visions will bury him. He can't look at death. Like all the Elysia babies."

Doctor licked his cracked lips. "He'll be back for some more soon. Drummers have to have their beat!"

"A drum, a drum, Old-Boy will come!" shrieked the women together.

All that night, Paul sat beside Rafe while the visions came.

"She's attacking me. She looks like one of them," Rafe cried. "Lily!"

"It's all right." Paul's beautiful voice. "It will stop soon."

"They rip men limb from limb. Heads go down the river singing. Roll down the river singing. Roll down the river still singing. Torn from him, torn from him."

"Rafe!"

"Her hair is a forest of fear. Her head looks as if it has been sewn to her neck. Her mouth sings blood. What powders her skin? Pollen? Dried blood? They will tear us limb from limb. Feel the wrench from the socket. The muscles pull and tear. The blood runs out of us. Mixing in a river of fear."

"Rafe, it will end."

"They can't see men together. It makes their teeth ache. Their molars and along the edge of the teeth there is a vibration. They would tear us limb from limb. See their veins big with blood. Their fingers like muscles. Let me back down. Lily! Lily! I have to have it again! Orpheus! They will tear me limb from limb!"

For days and nights they sat with him.

Paul played a flute and sang. Calliope played a small harp. They gave him water and filled the room with flowers. They slept there, taking turns on the couch, the other two curled on cushions on the floor by his bed. When he sat up, screaming, clutching himself, his eyes rolling, Paul and Dionisio held his arms and shoulders; Calliope stroked his forehead.

"A man's head floats down the dark red river. Just the head; the mouth is open. He is still singing!" he cried out.

At last, he was quiet, drenched.

"You look like you've been surfing, Rafer," Paul said tenderly, wiping away the salt water sweat from Rafe's temples. He remembered the first time they had gone out into the water together, Rafe catching drops of ocean on his tongue as they dripped from his hair.

> *I want to be with you*
> *Over the Under*
> *Under is stirring*
> *Voices in darkness*
> *Bones in the darkness*
> *Follow us everywhere*
> *Visions are blurring*
> *Follow you anywhere*
> *I'll lead you back from there*

Finally, it was coming to an end. A long descent. The Poet did not give up easily. It was morning and Paul sat beside Rafe on the bed. Rafe opened his eyes, focusing for the first time in a long time on Paul's face.

"How are you doing?"

"My head hurts. I'm hungry."

Paul tried to disguise his relief. "If that's the worst complaint you have, I'm leaving to do some work," he said with the old coolness.

Rafe grabbed Paul's broad wrist. "You better not leave me yet."

Paul looked into his eyes. "I'm not going to leave you. But I'm going to get you up out of this bed and start you drumming. You've been wasting my good time. We've got a show next festival and I'm getting another drummer if you don't show me you can play."

"I'm not ready to play yet, Paulo."

Paul turned to him, blazingly white. "You'll be ready," he said.

⌒

When Rafe entered the tent, the centaur lifted his heavy head and stared with caged eyes. Rafe turned from that gaze and saw the Old Clown on his unicycle.

"She died."

The clown's voice was raspy. "Did she go Under first?"

"I kept her here. I wouldn't let her."

"Well, at least that," the clown said. "Because that is the real death, down there. That's the death everyone fears. But they keep going down."

Rafe looked at the clown's cracked skin, more shocking, even, beneath white paint and framed in a flowery collar. "You're still here."

"Yes. They think I'm a freak. But I won't go down. And I won't leave Elysia. Which is my mistake. I've been here too long. Can't live without the sweet things."

"Well, then it's good you're staying. I'll do that, too." Rafe still could not imagine his body aging. Even after seeing Lily change. After everything.

"I doubt it," said the clown. "The babies say that, but when it's time, you go. You see yourself in the mirror with lines starting. You body slows. You see everyone around you like air. And you go. The earth pulls you."

"Not you."

For a moment, the Old Clown hesitated, playing with a strand of silver stars he wore around his neck. "I don't know why it's different," he said. "I'm stubborn. Maybe I enjoy abuse. But you can leave now, go to the desert. There might not be so much sugar and pretty things. You live simple. But you live together until you die."

Rafe saw land stretching clear to the horizon, dust, fires burning, faces in the firelight, some old, some young but soiled with the earth; he heard music, smelled embers, imagined stars. He had heard a story about a boy from Elysia who went under and brought some old ones up. Rafe saw their faces, blinking, terrified under their veils as they emerged into the sizzling, colored lights of Elysia on their way to the desert.

"Sometimes I think I don't need all this here. But then, other times . . . you get used to it." The flashing green mermaid outside of Lily's window, champagne-soaked cakes, playing his drums on the painted carousel.

"And you give up to get. I should listen to my own words," said the Old Clown. "The happier you are, the less you need."

"But I'm not happy. Maybe if Lily were here."

"Someone would make it easier. But you don't need anyone. You just need the drum inside of yourself," the Old Clown said, getting on his unicycle and riding away.

WISH

If I were a needle
I'd put love into your veins
If I were a needle
I'd take away the pain
If I were a wish
I'd grant myself to you
If I were a dream
I'd make myself come true

If I had a wish
I'd make the dying end
If I had wish
It would be childhood here again
If I had a wish
Love would be safe and pure

I have a wish
It's for a cure.

The Wish 5

After it was over, Rafe tried to remember Lily. But she was like a dream you know you have had and can't quite capture, though it still flickers in your head, beating its wings. In that hollow time, he found himself needing to be near Paul, to hear that voice.

They went to the Toy Store Tavern most days, Paul's eyes across the table pale, cool, starry as the eyes of the luminous, looming dolls, while he ate his cake and ice cream.

"What happened to Rafe-sugar-head?" Paul asked one afternoon when Rafe ordered only sparkling water.

"I'm trying to quit."

"You miss her a lot," Paul said.

Rafe told him how he couldn't remember her face, her voice,

all of her, touching his senses. Paul flinched a little, his shoulders alive in the white linen shirt he wore. Then he said, "If you haven't been able to remember your dreams, what do you do?"

"Sometimes I tell myself to remember before I sleep. But it hardly ever works."

"What about when you drum?"

"Sometimes then, and that's how Doctor gave me Lily back. When he heard how much I had to have her . . ." Rafe stopped, remembering. *I would find you dancing downtown.* Doctor sitting up in the booth, leaning forward, listening. "But now my music feels dead. Like it's coming out of my wrists and arms, not from inside at all."

Paul pushed aside the piece of layer cake drowning in chocolate ice cream. "Because you're broken inside like when you broke your arm. You have to let it heal, and then it will come back and she'll come back. But not like an Orpheus phantom ash-girl."

"I don't know if I want the memories without the senses, without being able to feel her and hear her. I don't know if I can stand it," Rafe said. Paul's shoulders twitched.

"You haven't played the way you need to."

"This isn't like an arm. It doesn't heal that easy, Paulo."

"Believe me, I know. You can lose someone a lot of ways. But then you can be alive again. You've got a music to play."

Seeing him then, lit up in the Toy Store Tavern among the huge dolls, Rafe remembered the first time he had heard Paul sing on the golden carousel chariot. Like a lion leaping through a ring of fire, like a sun god, Rafe thought.

> *Under underground*
> *You can hear the sound*
> *Music all around*
> *Don't lose what you've found*
> *Under underground*

Standing there, at the entrance to Under in the electric night, Rafe heard the women's voices calling to him, beckoning, beautiful in their desire and despair. He felt that if he went down, he could see her one more time—Lily. They would pity him, Doctor and the women; they had liked him in a way, he had felt that, as if he were connected to them somehow, and they would pity him, would give him one last beat so that he could see her face, hold her, speak to her and remember, always remember, after that. He would pay such close attention this time, to every detail, make up a rhythm in his mind that would bring her back later without the drug. He had had so few beats. Another wouldn't hurt. *Under underground.* And maybe they needed to see him again—the old ones, the addicts—see someone who had been Under and survived, come back up. He could help them, somehow, or promise them he would be back to help them.

> *Once I had a dream*
> *She taught me to believe*

Now I've lost her in a nightmare
But I'm going to find her somewhere
Even if it takes me Under

Down there, below him in the swirls of red smoke, Rafe imagined them calling out, and Lily among them, waiting for him to bring her back up, waiting for him, a ghost down there with all the other Orpheus visions who had been abandoned. An ash-girl ghost. He must save her.

Just as he was about to go down, he heard another voice from far away, but not from below him, not echoing up through the metal intestine of the tunnel, but clear, fiery.

If I were a needle
I'd put love into your veins
If I were a needle
I'd take away your pain
If I were a wish
I'd grant myself to you
If I were a dream
I'd make myself come true

It was Paul's voice. Rafe looked down in the hollow where the women wailed. It was like looking into Doctor's eye. Rafe turned and began to run through the cobbled streets towards the loft, his body drumming to the beat of Paul's song.

He burst into the loft and found Paul alone with his guitar. Paul looked up.

> *If I had a wish*
> *I'd make the dying end*
> *If I had a wish*
> *It would be childhood here again*
> *If I had a wish*
> *Love would be safe and pure*
> *If I had a wish*
> *It's for a cure*

Although Paul had never sung the song for Rafe before, Rafe knew it all. He sat down at the drums and began to play.

Together the golden man, the dark-haired boy-man gave birth to the child again. If they had ever dreamed of what life born of their two shuddering bodies would be, this was that dream made real.

Paul and Rafe drove up the coast to surf. As usual, it was a cold day, gray clouds drizzling strange rain. They ran down to the water, their bodies slick black in their wet suits. In Rafe's mind was the song Paul had written. *You are the ocean and you are the stream/you shine like water you are my wet dream.* The song transformed the clouded water, the waves becoming like giant petals peeling back as Rafe balanced inside them, riding to some perfect, pollen-filled center he never quite reached.

After they had come out of the water, eyelashes starring, noses running, bodies trembling with cold and exhilaration, they sat together on the sand, their boards propped behind them.

"Why doesn't anyone come out here?" Rafe asked. This far up, the water was murky but not poisoned with waste.

"They just don't care," Paul said, squinting out at the waves. "That's why it's poison all the way south. They don't mind if their sewers drain out in the water if they can have their circuses."

"But surfing's better than anything."

"People get bored so fast," Paul said, drying his hair with a towel. Rafe noticed how smooth the skin was on the nape of his neck. "And being out in the water reminds them, I think. That we're nothing compared to that force. That we're little and weak and mortal."

"Lily seemed to accept her mortality," Rafe said. "Maybe that's what I needed from her the most. But she accepted Under, too."

Paul slicked back his hair with his hands, still not looking at Rafe. "People accept Under because they don't want to face changing it. That would be too much work. I speak for myself, also. Ignorance is easier."

"But even individually. They could leave."

"If you go to the desert, you have to think about all those people down there. Their pain. If you even get that far with it. Most people don't leave just because they can't give up the sweet things. But you aren't addicted. I think you're just afraid."

Rafe recognized the challenge in Paul's voice, the challenge that had made him play his drums again, had helped him come off the Orpheus. "I feel like I'm too weak to do anything about it," he said. "What can I do? Go down and haul some old ones out? Against their will? It was their decision."

"We should try, really," Paul said. Now his voice was different, almost melancholy.

"I'm not good at convincing anyone of anything."

Paul turned to him. "What are you talking about? Your music is your power."

"What can that do? Besides get drugs?" Rafe bent his head, feeling the heat of Paul's gaze.

"Besides charm death! You have to believe in it as a healing force. Or a changing force, anyway. Then you can do a lot. You just have to work."

Rafe looked up. Paul's broad shoulders in shiny black, the perfect, angular jaw, the face even paler from the cold ocean, the hair drying to that shade of pale, whitish gold. Although it was an overcast day, Rafe imagined the sun gliding the water, blinding him, imagined the heat of the sun beating into him. He felt like some kind of plant grown in artificial light in a cage of green glass, a plant brought, for the first time, into the sun.

Wet dream, dream of me / You will free me make me clear / Wash away the need, the fear, went the song.

Rafe lifted his face to Paul.

DOCTOR

The ladies are hunting again and I like to watch the sport. Send out my hounds. To catch some stags.

I sit back in the dark Elysia club, watching, listening, like a king presiding over the hunt. My hounds have spotted the prey—two boys sitting at a bar—and they nose right up to them. One boy is that drummer, the other, his singer friend. Isn't it sweetness, how they sit together?

"How've you been?" Chloe asks the drummer. She's an evil one, that Chloe, a scabby thing.

"Fine," he answers. Cold. He should know better.

"Because we miss you down there. Are you still drumming?"

"Yes."

"So, who's this?" Shana asks, pointing to the blond singer friend.

The drummer isn't quite as much of a stupid ash-brain as he seems. He knows he'd better not push it too far. He introduces them.

But this Old-Stag, he won't say a word, just glares at my Lady-Hounds.

"You aren't very friendly, are you?" Chloe says to him.

"I don't think he likes girls talking to his boy," says Shana. Ha!

Leila speaks now. "What a waste. They're both so good looking."

"Except for his scars. I didn't know they allow that up here." Shana.

The drummer is aging over this. "Why don't you get out of here! What are you doing up here anyway?"

No, I was wrong. He's as much ash-brain as he seems.

Chloe tells him, "We come slumming. To meet live-boys. Those ash-boys don't satisfy. You know how it is. Probably how you feel about girls."

Ha!

"Go below!" the ash-brain live-boy drummer says.

My women leave them, but just for now—they'll be back. I hear them whispering together.

"They're penetrating each other."

"I don't like that kind of thing!"

"What are we going to do?"

"Chloe will think of something."

"Something beautiful. Appropriately beautiful."

Something beautiful.

KILLING TIME

You say it's obscene to say killing time
you call the words obscene, the act a crime
you tell me never waste it, let it be
but what you don't see is time's killing me

Moments between us are precious breath
moments nearer to our waiting death
each time I touch you more time slips behind
this is the game played by the killing time

I see the lines that wander in my face
I see the lines—a racetrack, like a race
you recognize a beauty in the lines
say they're the maps of all our love in time

You say it's obscene to say killing time
you call the words obscene, the act a crime
you say surrender to the will of time
a crime to kill it, time knows more than I

Killing Time 6

CALLIOPE'S VISION

Under underground. The streets beside the river. The water in the river is red. Three women are dancing. Beneath their knotted hair, I see their faces—snaky, peeling skin and glowing, milky eyes. I see the muscles in their arms and hands, also knotty. Their skin with scabs. They wear the skins of extinct animals, and they have teeth to tear.

Limb from limb. Two men—first one, then the other. Each woman holds a limb and pulls, wrenches with her knotted strength, with the strength of roots deep in the earth, roots muscling into the earth; this strength will tear the men. Limb from limb. The men scream. I hear their screams tunneling into my head.

Now I see the river. The red river. Yes, it is a river of blood.

What floats in that river? I hear singing. Haunting, beautiful. This singing could make trees dance. Who is singing?

There, in the river, I see. Two heads float, severed from bodies. Two heads float. Singing. One of the heads has golden hair and eyes of fire. One of the heads is dark-haired, pale, the eyes so full of water they are like pools of tears.

⌒

"Dionisio!"

"What?" he said, rolling over.

"I had another one!" she sobbed.

"No more visions, Callie. I can't take it."

"Dionisio! We have to go!"

He sat up, taking her in his arms. She felt suddenly small and broken. "It was just too much sugar, baby-girl."

They had eaten pastries for dinner with Rafe and Paul. Then they had gone back to the loft while the two men went for a drink.

"I saw them!" Calliope said.

"What did you see, baby?" He was beginning to feel a breath of fear on the back of his neck. Outside, a fireworks display whistled, popped, filling the sky with false color.

"These women. They were ripping at them, pulling them apart. And there was a river and singing and blood."

Dionisio grabbed her wrist and held her away from his chest, looking into her face. He had never seen her eyes like this.

"I saw."

"Callie, I bet they're right here."

Dionisio got out of bed, threw a blanket over his spare, dark body and ran barefoot down the hall to Paul's room. He opened the door and looked inside. The bed, set up like a stage along one wall of the velvety room, was empty. The gold sun clock above the bed showed it was hours past midnight.

Rafe's drum room was also empty.

"Let's go!" Calliope shouted.

"Where? They only said they were going for a drink. How are we supposed to . . ."

"Bring your guitar," she said to him, slipping on a cloak.

She would lead him through the streets under an exploding sky—her eyes like the aftermath of the fireworks, like smoke—her brother's face clear in her mind.

MAENAD

I say, "Those Same-Sex Penetrators!"

Shana and Leila and I are at the Boy-Club dressed like boys! And we wear hats too, so we can come up here above the ground. Don't we look handsome! Don't we! Doctor is at the bar with the collar of his coat turned up. I can see his eyes.

I can see the stage, and there they are. One tall, blond, and scarred. And that drummer, drums thudding beneath his hands like so many hearts. Those Same-Sex Penetrators!

Shana spits.

Leila looks at us. "What are we going to do, Chloe?" she asks me. Leila is an ash-brain.

But I know. I am the leader! "I want the scarred one to still be able to sing," I say, looking at him glowing on the stage. "I want to eat his body and leave his throat."

"We can rip them apart and hear the sounds. Muscles from bones, flesh from muscles!" Shana says.

Leila says, "Can I have the drummer? Can I have his hands and his sex and his heart?"

They don't see us. But even if they did, they wouldn't fear. They think their music sucks our power. But they are wrong! Wrong! The drummer is still weak. And with only the two of them, the music can't scald us, can't scar us or stop us. We wet our cracked lips.

The heads of these two will roll down the river. Down the red river. Singing. Still singing!

What's this? Who is this? That woman! That man! Where did they come from! They are heading for the stage.

> *You say it's obscene to say killing time*
> *you call the words obscene, the act a crime*
> *you tell me never waste it, let it be*
> *but what you don't see is time's killing me*

Shana bends over, coughing up mucus. Leila starts biting her arm. My head beats pain.

> *Moments between us are precious breath*
> *moments nearer to our waiting death*
> *each time I touch you more time slips behind*
> *this is the game played by the killing time*

We have to leave. Or we will be powder and ash. We have to leave! Doctor!

> *I see the lines that wander in my face*
> *I see the lines—a racetrack, like a race*
> *you recognize a beauty in the lines*
> *say they're the maps of all our love in time*

Doctor!

He is not answering. He sits cowering at the bar. He is staring at the girl and repeating something over and over.

What is happening? We must find the tunnel! Red river. River of blood. The music will slaughter us, will chase us like hounds on a stag. Ignite us and we burn. We must go down.

"Estrella! Estrella!" Doctor is moaning.

Ash-girls now.

Killing time.

DOCTOR

Estrella! Estrella!

It can't be. You are gone! You would not be up here. Estrella! My eyes ache, my tongue shrivels in my throat. We were in a desert once. We were falling into each other once. We were tasting the salt of stars. You kept pointing to the horizon. Something green; you wanted it. I couldn't see. You made me bring you here. Estrella! I thought I had forgotten you. And you are unchanged from when we first touched in the desert. Waves of heat glowed like layers of colored rock around us. Unmarked dunes. You found our son there. Had I beaten him with my own hands? That was the beginning. It was because I had changed! Estrella, I did not mean to grow old in this place. I did not mean to become what I have become. I wanted to find the essence of things—a green world, passion, fulfilled desire, love, life itself. Put them in vials. They are every color, like the flowers you wanted. Just snort, suck, inject them, and you can have whatever you want.

"Estrella! My garden."

I tried to make a doll that looked like you. Waiting for your return.

I go to you, reaching out to touch you as you stand there with your hands on the keyboard you wear slung around your body. I am staggering, the music piercing my skull. I am pleading your name.

"Calliope!" a voice shouts, warning, and you are pulled away from me.

"What did you say? Who are you?" you are shouting. "You can't be him!"

Calliope.

I search your face as you stand behind the boys. There is something different in your face. I back away, pulling my coat around me so you will not see my ruin. You are not my Estrella.

But you are mine. You were mine, ours. Calliope. And that boy with the drums. How would I have known? It was another life.

My children.

What have I done? Who am I? Skull rock. The looming bone face of stone that guards the desert, that is the desert.

Chloe, Shana, and Leila are real ash-girls now—burnt up, charred gray soot. Once, before they came Under to seek my magic to bring back their beloved ones, they walked above, fresh-flesh as the girl that is my daughter. Now they float on Elysia's neon air.

And where do I hide but down.

GIFT OF TIME

In this city of desire
Lotus blossoms float in bowls
Gold pulses at my wrists and throat
There is a fire and veils of smoke
I lift my veil——my face is scarred
Some violence done and something gone
You lie upon a pedestal
In my veins I feel your song
Run through my hollows like a river
Dark where it's still, when moving, shimmers
They will bind you in white linen
Heavy hands wrap up your limbs
And leave you in the darkness then
But your song remains with me
Radiance through the centuries.
Among the smoke and masks I wait
Emotion frozen on my face
I see you there, I recognize
The ocean world within your eyes
The lotus blossoms in your eyes.
I thought it was too late to speak
The passage of the centuries
It was too early then for me
I saw you in so many men
In the shadows, in the paint
In the words and in the songs
In the mirrors and the pools
In the masks of gold and jewels.
Until the day that you were real
Playing in the lilac light
Crystal flowers in your eyes

Love speaks through you like a child
Love speaks like an ancient child
Again, again, I say goodbye
Maybe always say goodbye
Waiting for some gift of time, waiting, waiting to unwind
The bandages that wrap us, keep us blind

Gift of Time 7

"*What am I* if that is my father?"

"He is my father, too."

"What does that make us? What monsters?"

"There was Mother. She raised us. And he wasn't always that way."

"Why? What made him that way?"

"They shouldn't have come back here to Elysia. He couldn't handle it. And in Under there are traps. He was a healer always. Maybe at first he thought he was healing people down there, giving them aphrodisiacs and even bringing back the dead. He didn't have Mother to guide him, and he didn't have himself anymore. This world had convinced him he was nothing, so he rotted away. He is not us."

"Calliope, we can never go down there. We might run into him."

"We will never become like him. He forgot himself. But you always have your music, Rafe. It will always remind you."

⟶

"I need to talk to you," Paul said.

Rafe was sitting at the drum table staring at the garden mural when Paul entered.

Paul sat down beside him. "Rafe, you know how I've felt about you. Since we started. Since we first played together and you knew all the songs."

"Paulo . . ."

"Just listen. You know all this. I mean, about Lily. I couldn't stand to see you with her, with any girl, anyone, but especially with her. I know how you felt."

"Paulo, it doesn't matter," Rafe said.

"Let me finish. It isn't that. I don't think this is right between us."

Rafe nodded, drumming softly on the tabletop.

Paul looked out the window of the loft. It was getting dark, and the carnival music was beginning to play.

"I've always felt like I've wanted to take care of you," Paul said. "But at first it was for me, what I could get from you, having you need me. But now it's different. I've never loved anyone this way."

Paul stopped, turning from the window to Rafe. Rafe saw that Paul was beginning to age. He knew now; it would happen to all of them. Soon, he too would have lines in his face, would have to make a decision.

"I think this place is bad for you," Paul went on. "You're not addicted to the sugar-trips like we are. Especially since Lily. I mean, we all talk about Rafe's Orpheus addiction, but we're all just as bad. You pretended Lily didn't have to die, and we all pretend everyone stays young and pretty. We won't even look at faces changing."

"So what are you telling me?"

"You've got to get out of this city."

Rafe wanted to touch Paul, touch the side of his face, the flesh that had been in torment once, years ago. "I'm not going to leave you," he said.

"You're just scared. But you know you have to. This place is Under. All of it. Elysia is Under, too. There is no real life. And as long as you're here, there's the temptation of Orpheus. And the chance of becoming like him."

Rafe knew Paul was right. After Calliope and Dionisio had found them at the club the other night, he had gone alone to the entrance of the tunnel again, stared down into that darkness trying to hear the voices, to imagine Lily's face. He had thought of the living skull who was his father. What had he recognized of himself in those starved eyes, those clinging fingers? Calliope dragged him away, back to the loft. But to go to the desert . . . "I don't know how."

"Just go," Paul said. "It's as easy as going Under; no one will stop you. Just get in your car and drive north. It's so simple.

People could go any time from here, but they just don't. They don't want to give up all the circuses and cakes to work. To live."

"What about you? All of you?"

"Maybe we'll meet you someday."

"But what if you get too weak and decide to go Under? What about the old ones?" Rafe thought of them shuffling in darkness. He wished he could go down and scream at them: "Get up. Get up there. Stand up. You still have spines. You still have legs and minds. We can learn from you." But he was not that strong yet.

Paul knew. "Leave for now. And then maybe you can come back for them. Come with your drum. Lead them all out from Under with your drum. You aren't ready yet to do that, but if you work hard . . . And maybe we'll be able to help you."

"By the time I'm ready, I will look like one of them. You won't be able to stand looking at me."

"By the time you look like one of them . . . I'm older than you, remember?" Paul said.

"You will always be beautiful, Paulo."

Paul touched his own face. "Maybe you won't see my scars anymore when I get old."

"We could all go to the desert!"

"I'm not ready yet, Rafe. I'm addicted to my carnivals," Paul said, getting up to stand by the window. He reached into his pockets and took out a handful of candy stars. The lights seemed to flash to the beat of the music that drifted up through the streets as Paul stood, eating his candy.

Rafe joined him. "You helped me. Maybe I could . . ."

Paul stared out at the Ferris wheel, his pale eyes reflecting the sparkle, his mouth dreamy for a moment. "Not yet. It's not time for me," he said softly. Rafe knew that Paul could not leave the carnivals, could not live in a place without sweet things. That Paul, like Calliope, Dionisio, Estrella, and like Lily, would rather live above in false light and pay in total darkness later than find something else, somewhere else, where light and dark took turns, reminding whoever saw the change that sometime everything would end.

Rafe buried his face against Paul's chest, and Paul held him, staring out the window at the Ferris wheel turning and turning like a ring of powerless, timeless suns.

⁓

"Old-flesh!"

Rafe, who was passing the circus tent with his drum, stopped to see what was happening. Three boys surrounded the Old Clown. They pushed him up against the side of the tent. One began hitting him, the clown's limbs becoming more and more like the limbs of a doll with each blow.

"Get out of here!" Rafe shouted, coming up from behind and dragging the boy off. The menace in his face turned to fear when he saw Rafe's eyes.

"Go!"

All three boys scattered down the cobbled streets. The clown regained his balance, holding onto Rafe's arm.

"You shouldn't stay here," Rafe said. He thought of Lily. How the clown had called her magic. "You should come with me."

"So, you're leaving?"

"I need to," Rafe said. "I'm not as strong as you."

"Stronger. If you leave, that's strength." The clown breathed heavily. Rafe tried to follow the lines in the flesh under the slightly luminous paint.

"It would be stronger to face it and do something about it here."

"Yes," said the clown. "Maybe you will."

"I wish you would come with me. They could probably use an Old Clown in the desert," Rafe said, smiling. He put his hand on the clown's shoulder, letting himself feel the fragile bones.

The clown looked at Rafe from under his starry hat. "No. But you be safe. And play your music. Travel, leaving parts of yourself everywhere. Make the trees dance. The rivers will sing for you as if they are full of the heads of poets," the Old Clown said.

As the clown walked away, back into the tent, Rafe began to beat on his hand drum. Lily, he thought. Let me see your face, let me hear you in the music again. The clown had left the flap of the tent open behind him and Rafe could see in to where the tightrope was still suspended. As he beat on his drum, the drum-shaped silver watch cool and ticking against his chest, Rafe saw a figure on the rope. A girl of air, her hair a cloud of flowers. He knew her. She was not an Orpheus vision. She was a memory. She was in his music. He would take that memory with him always like his breath.

PART 2

Persephone

LOSS' CHILD

Like the lovers in the frame
With no lines to divide
Our faces were the same
We felt the same inside

Now I never see your face
Now I never hear your voice
Now I do not merge with you
Now I do not have the choice

If I never see you again . . .
If I never touch your skin . . .
Touch your skin

Like a dreamer in the night
We both played all the parts
Where is it that you stop
Where is it that I start

Now I dream of giving birth
Now I dream of being born
You no longer stalk my dreams
Now I dream alone

If I never see you again . . .
If I never touch your skin . . .
Touch your skin

Like two in the same womb
We held on in the dark
Afraid to even move
Afraid to ever part

Now I dance to feel my legs
Now I sing to hear my heart
Now I paint to see my soul
Now I play all my own parts

If I never see you again . . .
If I never touch your skin . . .
Touch your skin

The start of faith is disbelief
Love begins alone
Ecstasy is loss' child
Ever still is never's soul

Loss' Child 1

It was like the time so many years before when he had fled his father's hands and run into the dunes, stumbling as sand cascaded beneath his feet, banks of sand driving him back. But he could not go back. His father had made welts rise.

Rafe was pretending that this second journey into the desert was different. He was much older now; he had a car, his drum, a backpack; everything had been planned. He liked to think that he was not running away from something this time, pursued by fear. Now he was going towards something.

Or was he? Was he only fleeing once again, afraid of his father, afraid of his own weakness when the dream was offered in a drug, the memory of those women scalded by Ecstasia's music, his feelings for Paul?

When they had said goodbye, Rafe had felt almost nothing.

He had been able to drive away without a backward glance. Now, as he drove, his whole spirit was wrenching in rebellion, trying to return to Elysia and find Paul's embrace. The constant solid heat of Paul's body, the startling softness of his lips, and the ache of his voice.

I must keep him with me, Rafe told himself, straining to see ahead into the darkness, trying to believe that the tears in his eyes were from this strain. The way I will keep Lily. All of them—Paul, Lily, Calliope, Dionisio, my mother. They are with me. In my music. He wondered if his spirit had fled from his body to return to the loft, a wraith of light wandering the darkened rooms, finding Paul's bed. And he, his body driving, was only an empty shell going off to find its desert grave.

No.

They are with me. In my music, he told himself, and kept driving. He gripped the steering wheel until his knuckles were the color of bone, telling himself it was only a way to stay awake.

They had stopped playing. They could not bring themselves to find someone to replace him—who could replace him?—so they stopped. They languished.

Paul wrote one song and showed the lyrics to the others, but he did not sing. His throat felt as if his vocal cords were torn. Perhaps they had torn that night when Rafe drove into the desert. That was the last night Paul sang, and it could hardly be called singing. In the morning he could barely speak.

They told themselves they would play again. It was just a

matter of time. But Paul's new song and all the other songs waited, unsung.

And outside the loft, Elysia chimed with clocks and jangled with mechanical toys, but there was no music.

"She will be a girl," Calliope said. "I can feel her."

"I wonder what she'll think of this place we're going to bring her into." Dionisio blew on the top of the empty wine bottle so his breath made a ghostly, echoing sound.

"Maybe she'll want to leave," said Calliope. "She might hate Elysia."

"All she'll know is this," Paul said. "None of us were born so deep in Elysia. And even so we're prisoners. If Rafe had been born here, he could never have left. He remembered the desert from before."

He looked at the shimmering garden mural. Calliope and Dionisio looked, too. They were all imagining themselves as children playing in the painted bowers, on the swings, swimming in the waterfall pools. And Rafe was not far away, somewhere in the desert. He was with them.

DIONISIO

There were always women around. My mother worked in the house at the edge of the desert with the glass towers like spears. Sometimes I wasn't sure if she was my mother. There were so many women there taking care of me and touching me. I grew up being handed from breast to breast and rocked in their arms. I liked watching their bodies slick with water from the baths, their feet steady and naked on the polished glass of the mosaic floors. I wanted to float among them and lose myself like a big bee feeding on the pollen between the petals. They let me roll on their satin beds and put perfume in my curls. In the courtyard they sang to me about a world where no one ever got old and flowers and fruit trees grew right out of the soil without artificial light and air. There were urns of ointments and fragrances, veils that hung in the door-ways' incense. The women bathed in sunken pools and dressed in kimonos and rose-colored crystals. They made a mixture of almond meal, honey, and dates for me to eat.

I hardly ever saw other children until one of the women came out of the desert with a pale, blond boy whose face was already hard. Paulo.

"What is the night made of? Black salt. Black crystal. Eyes." A woman sang the words he had murmured to her. "He is a poet," the women said.

I remember lying with my head in Jade's lap, her hands deep in my hair and the blond boy's words all around us. We were in a circle of music, hot house flowers, and candles, and the wall with the fresco of dancers protected us from the desert night.

Paulo and I rode on the back of the stuffed panther, and the women said that once creatures like that really lived, that you could even go see them in cages and that some were killed for cloaks. The panther wasn't like the centaurs in the circus or the harpy bird-women in the circus at the city's center. Even though it had glass eyes, I knew that when its eyes were real they had

been full of something so clear. Not the tortured eyes of mutations imprisoned in circus tents. Even if it lived in a cage, that
panther could see to all horizons. I imagined its eyes, and when
I met you, Calliope, I saw the way those eyes would have been.
You are my panther goddess. In that house there were great
beauties—women like every jewel. Emerald and Rose Quartz
and Diamond. My mother was so bright that men said their
teeth hurt to look at her. She blinded them. I grew up with
nothing but beauty. Then I learned what goes on down below.
The women went crazy as they aged. They moaned, reeling
through the rooms on the night before they were going to leave.
I clung to the stuffed panther, burying my face in its dusty fur.
I sensed that if the women could become like this panther, preserved in their beauty, they wouldn't have to leave me. They
were wishing for that. I felt their prayers materialize like spirits flooding the ruby-lit rooms at night. They didn't want to go
away. They'd rather have turned into glass statues of their most
gorgeous selves. When I learned that beauty changes and that
when it changes, vanishes below, banished, then I heard the
spirits raging. No beauty comforted me then. No brush of fingers or lingering scent or resonant laughter as the women gathered downstairs to be chosen, sauntered upstairs in their liquid
robes. I knew that when Diamante's breasts changed she would
leave here. Bijoux had found a gray hair reflected in her mirror.
My mother, Jade, had nightmares of burning her kimonos before she descended. Only when I drank the wine they slipped
me at the long gold table did I forget. We all forgot. Time stood
still, and I would be their adored, garlanded little boy forever.

None of them would ever leave me. My veins filled with the blood of the grape, and there would never be any sadness. We were all panthers—perfect, immortal, and glassy-eyed.

Only you, Calliope. You make me believe that I don't have to be scared of anything. Because a different beauty is born when you kiss me. It will go on and on forever. Even when we go below. If only you could keep kissing me all the time to chase away the cries. Now they no longer belong to the house of women. Now they are mine. My nightmares plead with me, "Follow Rafe into the desert, don't let yourself to Under."

Rafe, my brother, your sister and I are going to have a child. Maybe we'll come out the way you went. I want to see our daughter grow.

PAUL

I noticed the men that came from the desert to see my mother. They came swathed in cloaks; I couldn't see anything except their eyes. Then, as they entered the walled garden, they removed their clothes to bathe and I was aware of their smells and the density of their chests. I was aware of the way they moved, their muscled arms and calves.

The women said, "What a beautiful boy! Look at his eyes. What has he seen? Look at the tilt of his cheekbones, the tilt of his face as if he is always in communion with stars, as if the stars sing to him even in the daylight. Look at the color of his eyes as if winged creatures pressed opals to his temples. And look at his hands, his wrists, the shape of his shoulders already. Already he has bones like a small man. His eyelids are like doves."

The women said, "Listen to the words he sings. Is it true they are his words? Litanies. Hymns. Dark oceans. How would he know these things? Is he reborn, an ancient soul? Or did he hear things in his mother's womb, in the stirring of her tides? Is it just something in his body, in the way of his cells, his bone, his flesh? Does he hear the stars?"

They stroked my hair, they brushed against me, their hands lingered on me while they bathed me. Some of them looked at me and seemed afraid.

"He is only a little boy, a small child."

Somewhere inside of me, hidden among the songs celebrating the women, there was a dark song for the men. But I knew that the cool sparks of fire bristling along my limbs should be stilled. That it was wrong, somehow, forbidden. That somehow evil would come of it.

I wondered if out in the desert it was wrong. I thought of leaving the glass building, the outpost at the very edge of nothing, and going back to the place I had been born. In the desert, men could touch each other easily and understand it as a ritual to the stars, I thought.

But by the time I was old enough to leave, I was addicted to the glass garden and the fountains and the platters of iced rum cakes. I still wanted men, but I couldn't go out into the emptiness. So I went deeper into Elysia.

What will Calliope and Dionisio's child want?

What does Rafe want? Is he free now? Why did I tell him to leave?

"Tell us about Rafe, Callie," said Paul, but he knew she was already gone. He lifted his guitar and stroked its neck.

CALLIOPE'S VISION

It is night. The air is dark dust sage silence. Rafe sits alone on the sand before the skull rock. Its shadow consumes him. I have seen that face before; the face of the skull.

The desert takes our fears and nightmares and shows them to us. The jagged, gaping rock mouths that swallow us up, the accusing, vengeful giants with hollow sockets. They are alive in the desert. We cannot escape them as we do in Elysia.

I see my brother alone, sunburned, ragged, sitting on the hood of his car, the car that once brought us all out of the desert, gazing up into the face of his fear. I want to go to him, find him the way I once did, when he was a child weeping in the dunes. I want to bring him back with me, here, where he will be safe. But would he be safe here? Are any of us?

If I tried to tell Rafe to leave the desert, he would say, where is there to go? Here, at least life runs its full course. Butterflies can live here, although their lives are short. The most delicate creature of all can live here, in heat and desolation, and not in your manufactured city. I have seen bats and white owls and squirrels.

If I said, look, how can you live with those huge stones looming above you, every nightmare you have ever had? he would say, but the desert takes away my fear, absorbing it into itself, absorbing the poisons that have filled me and taking them into its landscape to be transformed into the gods of pain that can contain them. Here nothing is hidden. Here there is always the reminder of death, but there is also forever. Blood to bone to sand to stone to dust to weed.

I see my brother gazing into the eye sockets of the skull rock. It is like his father's face made vast and eternal. Although tears streak the dust that coats my brother's cheeks, he will not look away. He will not turn and drive back to our mirage city that floats above the underworld of our decay. And we cannot go to him. We are not like Rafe, who has his father's desert bones. I am like our mother, and Dionisio and Paulo are also children of Elysia. We would perish without our sweet things and our false green foliage. But Rafe must be away from what isn't real, or he may become like the man who gave him life, so ruined by this city that he lives death below.

The night falls and Rafe cowers in the skull rock's shadow, alone, wondering if we will ever come to him. His mouth is full of grit. He looks at his drums and wonders if they will ever bring life to this place. If trees will ever grow. If he will ever see green.

Somehow I know that if I am ever to see him again, if I am ever to help my brother, I must find the gardens.

There is a garden. It is not enclosed in greenhouse glass. It is not inside a glass museum. It is not carved or sewn or painted or dreamed or hallucinated. This garden is not in the desert and it is not beyond the desert. It is not in Elysia. This garden is not in the sky, floating in clouds.

I have seen it and it is underground.

At last he has learned how to create what our mother wanted. Our father has found the secret.

Under the earth, where we thought that there was only ash and stench, something else is hidden. Cascading fountains of amethyst and jade-colored waters shower down on acres of green, terraces of singing flowers. The foul air of Under cannot penetrate the canopy of verdant light. There is a dense jungle-like wilderness, ravines where healing herbs and livid mushrooms line the banks, and fields where butterflies and fireflies grow like flowers; there are grape arbors spilling fruit and apple orchards bussing with bee-sweetness; mossy, narcissus-starred grottos; bowers where the leaves play concertos; paths that lead through a lace tent of leaves past trees in the shapes of lions, lambs, and bears; plants that grow a myriad of eyes; silver cypress; weighty date palms; purple-blossoming jacaranda. It is the wealth of a world's gardens, here beneath the earth.

And everywhere, one figure stands guard, one goddess to whom all this is given. But it is too late. She is only a plaster cast of the woman who once lived. Again and again I see her face, peering through the passion flower tendrils, spouting the fountain's rainbow-colored waters, lining the petal-strewn pathways; she is the balustrade rails that overlook the water lily pools; she is the caryatids that support the vine-covered pavilion, repeated again and again, her perfect white body. She is everywhere and she is nowhere. The rose bushes form a maze that, seen from above, resembles her face. If only I could touch her. If only she could see this with me.

She is Estrella, my mother.

I follow the path of rough-hewn crystals lined with her white form. Her unseeing eyes, her silent lips. Suddenly I am afraid. It is as if she is inside each of these statues trying to get out, trying to call to me.

At the end of the path, the skull rock looms up. It is like that rock in the desert where my brother lies, asleep now, weary. It is a little smaller than that other rock, but it is the same grim mask of our father's face. And the mouth that cries its silent howl is not a mouth but an entrance into the stone castle where all these gardens germinate—into our father's very mind.

I wander the stone chill hallways, shivering. There is no hint of the garden there, no scent, while just outside I was drunk with sweet and bittersweet, floral and citrusy, heady, abundant scent. There is no sound of splashing, flashing waters and no warm air stirred with wings and pollen. I am back Under.

Sometimes as I wander down and down, I pass something that reminds me of Elysia. There will be a huge doll with clocks for eyes ticking in the darkness, her fat-cheeked plate-white face swiveling on her monstrous neck. Or a doll whose face is all clock—one giant clock perched on an enormous baby body. A juke box gilded with neon, hiccoughing some half-familiar tunes. A carousel calliope wheedling a haunting broken melody. But then these things are swallowed in the Under darkness, and the world above is gone again. And I keep going down to find him.

In some hidden laboratory cavern lit by smoking torches a man stands. Test tubes bubble with liquids. Vats boil and things float up, glimpsed for a moment—unspeakable and glossy in the torchlight. There is a stench. Here is where the essences of things are distilled, and from them are born the drugs that make us amorous, brave, even godly, the drugs that reveal gardens to us and bring back our beloved dead.

The man turns so that I see his face. His eyes are red and his mouth gapes as he reaches out for the thing he sees. Only he can see her. She is his goddess. None of the images of her, replicated hundreds of times over in the gardens, moves and sweats and fills the room with fragrance as she does now in his mind. She is so perfect. The way she looked when he left her to go Under. This is why he made the Orpheus, so that he could have her again. And he will inhale that substance until it clots in his blood and ruptures in his brain just to see her. He will take her with him to the gardens he has made and say, look, I have done it, finally, I made you what you wanted and now we'll never have to leave them. It will be like Eden, neither of us ever aging and this paradise spread before us.

But, she will say, what about you I only live in your mind now and you become closer and closer to death look at yourself when you are gone we will both be what I really am already.

And he will rage, no, no I will find a cure and we will live forever in this place.

It isn't real, she says. You must give it back up to the earth, where it belongs. You must give it to your daughter, our daughter. She can bring back the life that was lost.

Not to us, he will say.

He tears at himself until he bleeds. This is how the devils were made, he thinks. Wise and winged with love they roamed the earth, they were nomad healers touching away the burn and the rash and the poison plagues until they were cast down and, still feverish with their knowledge and power, why would they stop creating worlds? Why would they stop their burgeoning gifted souls from dreaming? And who was to blame if the dreams turned rotten and began to stink of death? He sinks his teeth into what flesh remains on his arm and calls Estrella, but she is only a phantom now.

In his sunken cavern castle our father waits, building the dolls and clocks and music boxes of Elysia, brewing and concocting the drugs that will turn the children into ash but give them all they ever wanted first, planting impossible gardens hoarded for a ghost, waiting for her to be real.

I feel my heart drying to bone, grinding down to dust, and I can hardly breathe as the blood becomes chalky in my veins. The husk of my heart will split, and I will become one of the dolls with clocks for eyes or one of the plaster casts presiding over paradise.

But I have no choice now because I have seen the gardens the way I saw my mother in my mind. Unearthly, endless, blossoming green. The gardens that will save my brother and my lover and my friend who is a brother and the child that is beginning to form herself out of the pulse that shuddered between my body and Dionisio's in our bed.

And I must go down.

⟶

Calliope's hands were on her belly when the vision faded. She could feel the stirrings of the cells that would become her daughter, and she breathed deeply, trying to allow the sensations within to bring her back. Here she was in the room with the gilded walls, the strings of candy lights. Dionisio dozed beside her, his arm flung over his face, his curls spread out on the pillow. Paulo was holding his guitar, his body expressing every mournful chord, face and shoulders tensed, knees bent, swaying. But there was no music. Calliope imagined his voice.

> *Like two in the same womb*
> *we held on in the dark*
> *afraid to even move*
> *afraid to ever part*

Someday he would sing again. Under was far below. She was safe.

And her brother?

Calliope knew these visions would haunt her forever if she did not go down. It was as if the man below was calling to her, come to find me daughter come see what I have made for your mother you are so like her you will see your face reflected in the water lily pools and taste the orchard fruits and languish in the scent of roses did you know that flowers and plants look like the part of the body they can heal bleeding heart for bleeding heart blood root for the blood that is why I always gave Estrella those dense white roses because they were so like her I would grow for you a more violet-tinged rose and what about the daughter inside of you what rose shall we cultivate for her. . . .

When Calliope was a little girl, she remembered seeing her father and mother dancing in the plaza under the stone horses with torches for eyes and mouths. He wore a parka of suedes and velvets, and Estrella was enfolded in his arms. Calliope remembered standing there holding Rafe's hand, watching them dance, feeling proud that she and her brother were children of such love. Her father with his leathery face, older than the other faces. He knew things. How to build things and make and change things. Alchemy. Estrella, Calliope, and Rafe were mesmerized by whatever came into their hands—toys and clocks, kaleidoscopes, mobiles. But he wanted to transform things. Gardens, he would say to their mother. If I could give you gardens. He was dreaming of going back into the desert where his freedom was—where he would not be chastised for time that had made his bones stiff and taken sheen from his eyes, his hair, and flesh. While his son was so perfect, a boy whom the city would adore for that. The desert where he knew the secret names of the gnarled cactus and the hidden fields where crystals grew, the hidden cave of bones, the way of bats in twilight flocks, the way heat stored itself in sheer slides of rock, the red-lipped mushrooms that let one see the life in everything, tremulous beneath the surface of everything, the incandescent buzz of cells hidden until you really looked and saw. If he could have remained in the desert. But she did not see gardens even when he gave her mushrooms to show her the way rocks breathe and sand whispers; those were not gardens for Estrella. And that is what she wanted. So he went with her, and each time anyone looked at him in Elysia, he must have felt it like a lashing across his shoulder blades. Old one old one with a wife and children so young. The son would grow up sheltered from the sun and wind, skin kept fine as a sheath of light with special oils and essences. All Estrella's love. And Rafe, he didn't have to give her anything, give up his world, his desert, strive to make her gardens, risk his life for her love the way our father did, Calliope thought.

"Callie, baby-girl."

Dionisio looked like a little boy rubbing his eyes with his fists, yawning. He knelt at her feet and lifted her white gauze skirt, kissed her bare knees, resting his curls in her lap. Paul kept playing his silent, sorrowful waltz.

"Where have you gone, Miss Calliope? Were you visiting with our girl child? Does she have my eyelids?"

Calliope, she asked herself, touching her lover's hair—soft, full, blown, fragrant as some black peony—where have you gone?

"Do you have candy?"

Calliope looked up. She had been wandering the streets blinded by more visions of Rafe in the desert. He was sitting on a rock in the blistering heat, wondering how the ashes of the dead could be scattered in a place without any wind. Remembering Lily's ashes swept into the waves beneath the pier as Ecstasia played. How could those ashes ever have been Lily?

Calliope's throat felt sandy and she wet her lips; they were splitting even in the humid air. She blinked at the pale girl dressed in a beaded web of silver lace, eyelids smudged with iridescent shadow. The child danced like a marionette, holding out her hand, her fingers somehow too long for her palm, dangling from it as if by string. It was strange how old Elysia's children seemed in their costumes and makeup, Calliope thought. Sometimes the youth that was so valued here was lost beneath the glitter.

"Candy?"

Calliope reached into her pocket and took out some of the chocolate wafers Dionisio loved. The little girl popped them into her mouth and closed her eyes for a moment, like an addict who has finally retrieved the drug. She skipped away singing to herself, "Butterfly flutter by, sweet meat meat sweet, sugar pie, pie in the sky."

Calliope touched her belly.

"What will we call you?" she asked her daughter. Will you be Estrella or Jade like your grandmothers? Will you be our Verdigris or Emeraude or Primavera? Primavera. Will you grow up gnawing on candy, addicted to the sweetness you savored in your mother's milk? Will you want to sing and dance on a stage wearing pretty clothes? Will you thirst for the quenching scent of flowers and find them false and somehow dead when you bury your face in them? As if a part of you remembered (you couldn't really remember) the way they once grew out of the ground? Will you dream of lawns that become waterfalls that become rain forests? Will you go Under someday with a placid look on your face, Dionisio's drunken smile, my blind eyes, shrugging your shoulders saying, "It is my time," or will it infuriate you—the thought of hiding your face as it grows marked by time? Will you head for the desert like your mother's brother? Primavera.

Spring always followed winter in a time when there were seasons, Calliope thought, wandering past a bar where people dressed in kimonos and high black wigs sat on pillows drinking sake and staring out the glass walls into the damp seasonless night.

"Flutter by butterfly meat sweet sweet meat sky in the pie." The child's song echoed in her mind.

Then she saw the flower.

Somehow having wedged its way up between the cobblestones it was not a hot house flower and it was not made of organza or damask or tulle.

"And this is not in my mind," Calliope whispered to herself, feeling her skin grow taut and chill, "although I saw this once, in my mind."

This flower—so white—had her mother's face; it seemed to contain Estrella's soul. The sulphurous rain would come down on it. Elysia's air would choke it. Calliope knelt to touch the petals as warm and supple as young flesh.

If flowers can heal what they resemble, why didn't she have this to give to her mother when she went down the first time? She had gone empty-handed, and it had been too late. She had sat watching Estrella perish until there was nothing left but the plaster cast at the foot of the bed, waiting like a cage, and Rafe leading Calliope away. She should never have let their mother go down at all.

Our mother would be alive, today, Calliope thought—let herself think it for the first time.

But where? Not in Elysia. Not in the desert.

I must make something else for you, Primavera, she thought. Something Estrella did not have.

The man knew how.

Calliope bent to smell the flower, imagining what it would feel like to pull hard enough that the shredded veins of roots would release their dry, cramped grip from the earth. But she would never; a flower growing outside in the earth was rare and must be guarded, sheltered. She knelt beside it and put her face among the petals so that a powder pollen sifted onto her cheeks.

It was too much.

She wanted this more than she wanted Dionisio's body at the moment when he stroked her open, the moment before he entered her—how strange—more than she had wanted to go find Estrella, even. As much as she wanted her daughter to grow up somewhere better. She could feel the sensation of the roots tearing, earth loosening, and the flower her own.

Voices called to her from the flower's center, or was it from deeper down beneath the cobblestones?

> *The start of faith is disbelief*
> *Love begins alone*
> *Ecstasy is loss' child*
> *Ever still is never's soul*

It was Paul's new song, the way she had imagined it, an electric waltz. Calliope gripped the stalk and pulled. And bled; she had not seen the thorns. Blood trickled down her arm like the veins in marble, like her own veins exposed, and as she stared at it, the voice expanded, freeing itself from the throat of the flower's stem. When she looked back, the flower was gone.

A smoke, a vapor of flower apparitions, enveloped Calliope as she followed the voice down.

At the riverbank the old subway cars stood rusting, their windows shattered. Graffiti was scrawled in black spray paint across their dinosaur bodies.

Loss' Child, the graffiti said.

Who had heard their song? Calliope wondered. She was looking for the gardens. Or at least for the stone castle with its jawlike door. For her father.

But there was nothing.

There was only the oily river. There was the shore heaped with bones and rusted machine parts and clotted masses of something that looked like weeds. And these ghostly subway cars in which one light burned, one figure moved back and forth dreaming of all the worlds he could create with an injection, a powder, or a pill, his mind like a train racing through the subterranean city where even the trains were only broken shells.

The figure looked up and stared out the cracked glass at Calliope waiting on the shore.

When their eyes met—were those eyes in his head or emptiness?—she stepped forward. She entered the train, half expecting it to lurch off down the ancient tracks. It was a tomb. She went to meet him.

"You look just like her," he said.

Calliope watched him surrounded by the huge dolls in various stages. Some were just heads, others wigged and painted, attached to bodies. One was finished, her fine teeth sharp and precise enough to bite meat with, her eye sockets set with small clocks. The doll was the only thing that Calliope recognized from her vision. Yes, it was remarkable, lifelike enough to make one shudder—a real girl with hair and skin, whose eyeballs had been traded for time.

Calliope remembered, suddenly, another doll. A man, this man, but different, holding out a doll to her.

"Don't be afraid, Calliope. I made her for you. What will you call her?"

And she had screamed, "She is watching me. Who is she? Mama."

"Don't be afraid."

And now he spoke again, this man who had been her father, who now lived in a tomb train beneath the earth.

"Why have you come back? You ran away from here. You didn't think you needed anything from me. You destroyed my ladies."

Calliope tried not to look away from the ridge of bone that was his face. It was like looking at the skeleton of her own face or Rafe's exposed, none of Estrella's lushness.

"Ladies? Demons," she said.

"Demons? They were just like you when they came down here. Pretty ladies seeking something."

Calliope tried to control the tremors in her body.

"You're proud like me," the man went on. "Not like your brother. He has Estrella's hunger."

"You're wrong. Rafe went back to the desert."

"So he did take after me a little." The dry laugh. "And you? Maybe the resemblance to your mother is more than in those eyes and lips. Why did you come down? What desire is greater than fear?"

Calliope felt the doll eyes watching her. Suddenly, all the dolls looked like small, bloated versions of Estrella.

"You want Orpheus to bring Mommy back. You know I created that drug to bring her back. It works very well. Or . . . you want something to keep your boyfriend at home? Aphrodisiacs for pregnant girls. Venus Trap. That's an easy one."

"I don't want your drugs," she said.

"Oh. Too pure. No drugs for Estrella's daughter. Right."

"I'm your daughter."

"Yes. You must want something to come down here calling me Daddy."

"Please." It was a plea to memory more than to him. She tried to remember the magician giving her dolls and musical instruments, blowing soap bubbles for her, dancing with her balanced on his feet, the bulk of his arms as she nestled against his chest, the desert brown of his skin. How different he was now—bleach-bone, underworld.

Calliope knelt and closed her eyes, trying to see the man, her father, before his ruin. And maybe he would see her as the child he had brought from the desert. She felt dizzy, grasping for hope, for the vision that had carried her here.

"You can make gardens," she said. "You are our father and you loved our mother. Please help me bring back the gardens."

He laughed again. "You think I can do that? Do you think I'd be down here rotting if I could make the paradise you are looking for?"

"I saw it." She was almost weeping. There had to be something. Her visions had never misled her. Or was it just that her desire had made her see the green? Her desire to heal the scorched plains where her brother wandered. Her desire to give her daughter a perfect world. The same desire had drawn Estrella to Elysia and destroyed their father.

What had she done? She could have gathered up Dionisio and Paulo and gone to find Rafe. Together they could have worked. They could have made some world. At night by the fire she could have told Primavera about the gardens of her dreams. Primavera would be the green. It would be enough. She would go back up. What had she done?

But the man, Doctor, was laughing, throwing back his head, his throat muscles like ropes being pulled taut with each strain of breath. "So your visions aren't infallible? Don't worry. We'll fix you up. You want gardens? We'll get you some. Persephone. Isn't that a pretty name. Persephone. My latest creation. If only Estrella could have tried her. If only I had thought her up while we were out there."

And he was cracking open the blood-colored husk of the orb. And he was prying apart the insides. And he was ripping the small, bright kernel from the honeycomb sheath of skin encasing it and he had Calliope pressed against the wall, her jaw forced open.

Spring was in her.

CALLIOPE ON PERSEPHONE

My lover, your father, stands with one hip thrust out. One hand reaches to pluck the fruit from the trees. He only needs to hold out his hand and the plums will drop—the color of his curls and the flavor of his lips. Sleek and dense as flesh. When I look at his bare rib cage I see the shadows of space between the ribs where my fingers will fit when he plunges into me.

As Paul stands on the bank playing his guitar, the flowers turn to catch his eye, their faces following him to feel his heat, opening to him. His skin is smooth, radiant goldleaf; all the scars are healed; he shimmers. He is laughing as Paul has never laughed, music all around him, and lions as tawny and sinewy as he is pace at his feet with small boys riding on their backs.

My brother splashes in pools full of water lilies and fish that pulse with light like candles. His hair is black as violets. The willows bend to stroke him with their fall of green. They feel their roots moving in the earth—born dancers who have never danced before.

In this garden the winds blow vein-blue and lip-rose. The winds are lovers caressing, tumultuous, swelling, their mouths crammed with petals. See how the flowers are women smiling mystery in their embroideries, a tapestry. See how the flowers beat like hearts, open and close like lips, bodies moist with love.

My daughter, this is your garden. These bowers and arbors, these fountains of wine. These flowers like constellations, hot and bright as suns on their stalks. These dancing trees and flowers that sing. This sky of leaves, plums, peaches, grapes, apple blossoms. All this green is yours, Primavera. You will never have to go Under.

DIRGE

Have I forgotten no I remember
though I have tried to burn it to embers
the night when the one in the skeleton mask
ripped at my heart while he kissed my mouth
the night when the one with the fingers that pry
opened my rib cage and buried inside

There in the city that denies destruction
all of them waiting for love's resurrection
so many children in so many rooms
so many boys in the carnival suits
so many girls await their retreat
all armored and masked out on the streets
girls in their rooms, a mysterious glow
flickers of dream on their half-shadowed brows
are they awaiting the return of love
or has despair wrenched them, fastened like gloves
to their hearts in the tapestry dark
in the cupid-filled, dizzying, mirror-bright dark?

There in the city that denies destruction
all of them waiting for love's resurrection
and all of them—blind girls and boys who have seen
our brothers vanish and never be men
sisters get ready to go down below
the city vampire-like and seraphic, both
children, too pale, watch shooting stars
as they're led past the hole in the earth to the bars
children with everything there for their eyes
too much for such pallor, such size

But something's begun again, feel it exploding
into a dawning, a rushing unfolding
listen to rain and the rooms that resound
with the song and the wail of a heart as it sounds
out the sweetness of angels who live in museums
and the stark echo chambers of dark mausoleums
waken, awaken, beside you in song
not till the end will we know and belong
still I will feel the thirst and the shimmer
desiring you, fired by you, blinded by glimmer
where did you come from, this city that strikes
out at them all in the electric bright night?
wakes them with questioning song-rustled light
always the waltz and never the dirge
tell me your name before I emerge

Dirge 2

CALLIOPE CREATURE

Ring around the rosy pocket full of posy ashes ashes we all fall down red rover red rover send my brother Rafe over miss mary mack mack mack all dressed in black black black with silver buttons buttons buttons all down her back back back cinderella dressed in yella went upstairs to kiss a fella made a mistake and kissed a snake how many doctors did it take spanish dancer turn around spanish dancer touch the ground humpty dumpty sat on a wall humpty dumpty had a great fall all the king's horses and all the king's men couldn't put humpty together again once upon a time happily ever after my name is Calliope I was born under the sign of the virgin my mother's name was Estrella my father is called Doctor he was not always called that although I don't know what he was called his face is harsh I have seen those harsh bones in my own face

and in my brother Rafe's I try to see Estrella's softness her
cheeks her lips my father lives below the first boy I ever kissed
chased me with a jump rope and caught me in the schoolyard
the first boy I ever let make love to me was Dionisio I took off
my dress for him and I imagined the way the animals used to be
before they vanished because he was sleek and sinewy like I
imagine them and licked me with his tongue and has hair like
fur I live with Dionisio he is my lover we are always in each
other's arms as if to find something as if to escape something this
means that I love Dionisio our other friend is Paulo I love him
too but in a different way than I love Dionisio Paulo sings while
I play keyboards and Dionisio plays bass sometimes I imagine
what it would be like to make love to Paulo because he is so
handsome and full of strange powers but he never touches
women although I think I remind him of Rafe and I think he
loved Rafe love love love I think that word a lot I love Dionisio
and Paulo and I loved my mother Estrella I used to love my
brother Rafe but now he is gone so I can forget about him I
don't love my father but when I think of him I feel something
tighten in my chest and I never feel that when I think about anyone else but I don't talk about my father when I was a little girl
he would take me with him to get ice cream and give me dolls
he made and sometimes we'd miss dinner and Estrella would be
mad but I didn't care because I was with him and that made me
the most important and the most beautiful because I was so
young and he also taught me about flowers all the different
names of greenhouse flowers heliotrope begonia nasturtium
hollyhock gladiola larkspur peony star-gazer tiger lily he also

knew about herbs St. John's wort burdock calendula tansy yarrow he had vials full of colored things if your head hurt or you turned an ankle or you were cold or if your heart was broken he would say but I was too young to know about that and now I can't remember here above the ground Ferris wheels go round and the dance of clowns a carnival—this town only a playground stay young stay up above before it takes you down I dream of a place where wings fill the sky we dance like an earthquake drink ambrosia wine somewhere in the dawn light I would find your kiss I would not awaken never shut the pages closed on this I want to be with you illness beneath us not hear the stirring chill in the darkness voices in darkness not hear them cry for air visions are blurring follow you anywhere I'll lead you back from there moments between us are precious breath moments nearer to our waiting death each time I touch you more time slips behind this is the game played by the killing time waiting for some gift of time waiting waiting to unwind the bandages that wrap us keep us blind like the lovers in the frame with no lines to divide our faces were the same we felt the same inside have I forgotten no I remember although I have tried to burn it to embers always the waltz and never the dirge tell me your name before I emerge under underground underground

My name is Calliope. My mother, Estrella, died underground the way we are all supposed to die. I saw her before she was placed inside the plaster cast that hides the deterioration of flesh. I was the last thing she saw, before. My brother Rafe rescued me from underground or I might have stayed there forever. I might have had them make up my plaster cast right then. I might have waited in my mother's bed till I perished and was hidden inside a body that will never wrinkle or rot. But my brother Rafe reminded me and brought me back.

My brother Rafe used to play with us in our band, Ecstasia, but Rafe has gone away. He has gone to the desert so that he won't have to go underground. While we will stay lovely and preserved by Elysia's climate and fine oils and luxuries, Rafe will weather and age soon. In a way, we——Dionisio and Paulo and I——will always be young because when we do finally age we will just disappear below. But Rafe will continue to crumple into an old man under the desert sun. He will not be buried in a plaster form that shows him at a peak of flawless beauty. He will probably not even have a stone to mark his grave.

I wanted to help Rafe because he is my brother. Rafe is another person I love. That is why I wanted to help him. I wanted to find him in the desert and make water spring out of the earth. I wanted to sing to the sky until it turned beautiful colors and rain came down. I wanted to be able to plant fields of never-ending green. So I went Under to see Doctor.

Doctor is the wisest man I have ever known. I am afraid of him. But he is my father. He knows how to change the earth. So I went to him.

I asked Doctor to help me so that Rafe and Paulo and Dionisio and I wouldn't have to die in the brutal desert or vanish underground. I wanted what my mother Estrella had wanted but more. I wasn't happy enough with Elysia's pretty lights. Also, I knew I had this child inside of me.

This child is Dionisio's child. But it will never be born from me. Doctor told me this. One reason I went Under was to make the world better for my daughter. But she will never be born. I am not supposed to tell anyone that I know this.

Now that I know my child will not be born, now that I have gone to see Doctor, now I know that I will not be so proud as to try to make the desert grow green. I will not try to rescue my brother from the desolate world he has chosen. I will enjoy the gifts of Elysia.

My name is Calliope. I used to have visions, but now I don't. The only thing I know about the future now is that I will never try to leave Elysia to help Rafe because he chose his life, and I will never have a child because I can't anymore. My body looks the same but is somehow different.

I will go back to Elysia where I live and play music with Paulo and Dionisio and lie in Dionisio's arms in the night and eat the cakes and drink the champagne and go below when I am supposed to go below.

But maybe I will never get old the way Paulo and Dionisio and Rafe will all get old. Old and ugly. Maybe I've changed. I won't tell anyone this, but maybe I am going to be young and beautiful forever and ever. That was what my mother wanted. That is what everyone wants. Maybe my father knows something about this. Maybe it has something to do with the reason the baby will never be born from me. Maybe I am perfect now.

⌒

She looked just like Calliope. But her skin and hair and nails were manufactured. Her heart was a clock.

And no one would have known.

Even her lover would not have known the secret of her emptiness. Doctor had created his daughter once again.

It began long ago when he went underground. He could not stop dreaming of Estrella. How he wanted her. The drug Orpheus was not enough. He gave it to the children instead, the ones who came seeking their parents, their lost lovers. Let them turn to ash. He would make something better for himself. Not just a drug. He, the master, would make a woman. He would make Estrella.

The dolls came first. He had made dolls before, above. It was almost funny now to think of it. He had made dolls for his daughter Calliope as a diversion from the work of creating potions. Everyone in Elysia loved the dolls. False children, machinery dressed in a substance exactly like flesh. They walked and spoke. The first one had made Calliope cry. She was so real.

"She's watching," Calliope had screamed.

Estrella tried to explain and finally had to take the doll away. Later, Calliope loved that doll. What had she called her? Primavera? Primavera was the beginning of many all leading up to one. And the one was so complex that she was no longer a doll. She was almost a living creature.

But the Estrella creature was incomplete. She had her insides, engineered to perfection. Every hair was on her head; her skin had pores, her irises reflections, her limbs motion. But, soulless, she was nothing to Doctor. She was not Estrella. Estrella had perished.

The Estrella thing waited in the back subway car looking like

Estrella when Doctor had first met her. Or like Calliope. Exactly like Calliope without a soul.

And now Doctor went to where his daughter lay in a stupor, drugged with gardens, a narcotic spring goddess with pomegranate lips and eyelids that fluttered over petal visions. He touched her dark hair, her feverish cheek. He lifted her in his arms, carrying her through the train, her head thrown back, and he whispered to her, "Sleep, daughter, dream Persephone. Prosperina. Presephassa. Every garden you have ever wanted."

He would wire her to the thing and charge it with her electricity, give it her past, her thoughts, everything. Then he would let the thing go above ground to keep the boys who loved Calliope in line. He wouldn't need it anymore. Now he had his daughter.

The Estrella was moving her arms and chattering, "Doctor Doctor Doctor."

She was awaiting, finally, life.

"Where have you been?" Dionisio cried, taking Calliope in his arms. She felt cold and her eyes were glazed. "You've been Under."

She pressed her head against his chest. As if trying to capture his heartbeat, he found himself thinking. What had happened to her down there?

"Calliope?"

Then Paul stormed in, almost crackling with anger. "You're pregnant. How could you do that? Calliope. Look at me."

She buried further against Dionisio. "It's all right, " Dionisio said. "She's back."

Paul sank into some tapestry cushions. "First she goes. Then Rafe. Then she goes again."

"You sent Rafe away," Dionisio said. "You told him to go to the desert. If he hadn't left, Calliope wouldn't have gone Under again."

"You went Under?"

"Look at her, Paulo. Where else? Look at her eyes."

"I know. I know." Paul absently tore threads of gold fringe off a cushion. "We thought that's where you went. We were about to go down to look for you. How could you have gone there with the baby?"

"She's not your baby, Paul," Calliope murmured, her voice muffled by Dionisio's chest.

"You're right. She's your baby. And Dionisio's. What is wrong with you? You both might never have come back."

Calliope began to sob, raw, dry gasps. Tears did not moisten the nubby, dark-amethyst silk of Dionisio's shirt.

"Leave her, Paul," Dionisio said. "We've got to take care of her now. She's like ice." He lifted Calliope in his arms—how heavy she felt; the baby must be growing—and carried her to their bed beneath the arbor of silk morning glories. The sheets, the whole room, were so saturated with Calliope's aura that no one, not even Dionisio, could have known that this creature lacked it. Would not have known that this creature's soul was only a copy of Calliope's soul, as false as the morning glories that never withered or shut their petals to the night.

This new Calliope inhaled deeply of the light and fragrance that the other Calliope had left behind. She was hungry for it;

she was starving. When Dionisio had held her she had known something of real life.

CALLIOPE'S VISION

All the gardens have died now. They are choked with weeds, burned, dried up.

Dionisio crouches beneath the skeletal fruit trees; hallucinations of gaping-mouthed plums are taunting him.

Paul touches the sunflowers, and they flame up as if his fingers were fire. For a moment, the sunflower fire is like an incandescent garden and then it is only burning stalks and petals and then it is scorched remains.

Rafe lies on his belly trying to drink from the pool, but all the water has been soaked into the sand and he is parched, prone, almost lifeless. The bones of animals are heaped beside him on the bank.

The winds are diseased lovers coughing and sputtering ash. Spring is poisoned. She is a goddess with a whip of thorny vines and blood on her hands. She rides a black steed whose bones show through his flesh.

Where is Primavera? Where is my daughter?

I see myself but it is not myself. And I am—she is—lying in Dionisio's arms. He is stroking her face, he is whispering my name. But it is not me. And I cannot tell my lover that it is not me he holds.

How can Dionisio not know? He does not know because she

is so like me. But she does not have this heart. And she does not have this child within her—only a hollow curve of manmade flesh where the child should be.

Dionisio and Paul will feed her wine and jams and sugared violets. They will comb her hair and fasten it with my abalone combs. They will play her music and sing to her. Without me and Rafe, they will still be Ecstasia for her, to save her, sharing with her the music that once was part of all of us like a child.

> *But something's begun again, feel it exploding*
> *into a dawning, a rushing unfolding*
> *listen to rain and the rooms that resound*
> *with the song and the wail of a heart as it sounds*
> *out the sweetness of angels who live in museums*
> *and the stark echo chambers of dark mausoleums*
> *waken, awaken, beside you in song*
> *not till the end will we know and belong*
> *still I will feel the thirst and the shimmer*
> *desiring you, fired by you, blinded by glimmer*
> *where did you come from, this city that strikes*
> *out at them all in the electric bright night?*
> *wakes them with questioning song-rustled light*
> *always the waltz and never the dirge*
> *tell me your name before I emerge*

Just as Dionisio and Paulo and I healed Rafe, sitting at his bedside, bringing him back with music, my lover and my friend will now try to bring me back. But it is not me. And their songs and their hands and their love cannot reach me here, cannot free me.

What will their love do to the creature who wears my face? Will they see, finally, that she is as lifeless as the clock-eyed mechanical dolls serving drinks in the bars? Will they never know that she is not me but grieve because they cannot return me—her—to health? Grieve because our baby will never be born from her? Or will, somehow, their love give this creature a real soul of her own? Even, give her a creature-child? A Primavera-doll? Will Doctor take my child and send her up to be raised by his creation? And I will be left here in this train beneath the earth. But at least, then, Dionisio and Paul will not suffer anymore and will not be in danger of coming down to seek me out.

Maybe I am not Calliope at all. Perhaps the real Calliope has gone back to Elysia, and I am the phantom doll dreaming of hell's gardens.

While somewhere in the desert Rafe sits at the edge of a dry ravine, a bed of sand. Around him, the rocks are giant, gaping-mouthed fish, whales, schools of dolphins and womblike shells; the cactus like huge seaweed.

I am in the bottom of an ocean, Rafe thinks. An ocean without water. Isn't that what the desert is?

His hands beat on the drum he holds between his knees. He is trying to make the rain come. He is imagining an oasis of date-laden palms. He is imagining that the ravine is full of bubbling water.

But the ravine is dry.

A stone man squats at the bank, bald, heavy-haunched, massive. His hands are cupped as he tries to drink. Rafe sits beside him. The man will squat there forever, monklike, thirsting, waiting. Rafe looks at him and thinks, is this what I will become out here? Alone without my loved ones. Will I become stone?

How can I ever go to him? There is no green to bring, and now I can never even see the garden of his face except in dreams.

Now I dream a child emerging from my body. Why didn't I realize before? She is the spring. She is all we needed to make the desert green. She and our love and music. But I went searching for something else, and now I may never see her beneath the sky; she may never even see the sky. I call her Primavera, and there may never be a spring.

CALLIOPE CREATURE

I am supposed to have a heart inside my chest, but all I have is a kind of clock. This man does not know that. He holds me as if I had a heart. He tells me about how we met, how I took off my dress for him. He tells me about how I make him high and that he hopes our daughter will look like me. I have nothing to say to him. I press my face against his neck.

This man has dark curls and smells of fruit and smoke. He holds his gleaming bass guitar and plays for me. He swoons with music.

The other man, the tall, blond man, sings in a throaty voice. He looks right at me as he sings as if he is trying to penetrate me with the words and melody. He does not know how hollow I am and that his music will die in the empty chamber where my heart should have been.

But when I see them—these two men—something strange happens to me. It is as if the real Calliope is with me. She is putting her hands on her abdomen where the baby waits. She is saying, "Love. Do you know what that is?" I shake my head. Looking at her is like looking at a mirror, but she is so different. She is so full.

"Love," she says.

I am hollow.

Then I look at the men. The dark-haired one closes his eyes, wets his lips as he plays. His hips pulse against the instrument. The other, taller man looks as if he is about to weep with the strain of singing. I want to dance. Calliope would dance. She would play music. She would make flowers grow. How can I be here in her place? When will they see that I am not ill, sickened by my journey underground? When will they see that I *am* Under? Barren.

"Calliope," says the dark man who is my lover. "Come back, baby-girl. Where have you gone?"

He does not know that I have never been with him. I can never come back.

⌒

Two births were taking place.

One was under the ground. In that darkness, in that motionless train, Calliope lay on the floor moaning. Her legs were spread apart for the child to emerge like a small tree. Yes, it felt like a tree in a storm exploding, the pulse of stars, spring cracking awake, crocus through the sheaths of ice.

Doctor delivered the child. His nose and mouth were covered with a thin white cloth that clung to his bones with each breath. His hands were gloved—rubber and blood. Only his eyes were exposed. But what did they say? What does darkness say to light, soil to sky, death to life? Part of him was remembering with a tenderness he would not have thought possible. Part of him wanted to assert itself against that thing he could not ever really touch—that light and air and blossoming. Wanted to keep it, crush it, pulverize it into its essence—chips of crystal and whispers of pollen, radiance and brilliance. But that wasn't it. His rubber-gloved, blood-gloved hands were shaking. What drug could do this? What machine could become this? Not just the vision or the mechanism but something more, conceived of egg and sperm, forming into life in his daughter's mysterious womb.

He would hold her in his hands—his daughter's daughter. He would learn something. He would begin to understand. His own creation was walking above with no child inside her.

And yet, meanwhile, the other Calliope was having her own birth. While the real Calliope sweated and screamed Primavera into the world, the thing lay in Dionisio's arms, listening.

He was telling her about their life. It was like a great feast, she thought, like an orgy of beauty. They were dancing in the arboretum, they were drinking wine and wearing wreaths in their hair. There were mechanical dolls everywhere and people dressed as dolls.

How strange, she thought, that these people, who dream and bleed, value creatures that don't. I am one of those dolls. What would this man think if he knew? He likes the mechanical dolls to serve him champagne ices and for his lovers to dress up as one of them. But if he knew, he would fling me away against the wall where I would break.

Still, there was something about lying in his arms. She could almost feel what it would be like to be Calliope. His love was entering her. Maybe she had a heart, after all. It was as if Dionisio was reaching inside the cage of her chest with every word and winding up the mechanism that was her heart. It was as if he was injecting some blood-balm into her, into the thin, hollow cords that imitated veins.

"Dance with me, Calliope," Dionisio whispered. "We'll dance slow so we don't upset the baby."

In the other room, Paul was playing his waltz. Dionisio lifted the Calliope in his arms. She collapsed against him and he moved with her, his hand pressed against the hollow of her lower back, his eyes scrutinizing her face. It was as if he was trying to will her back to health, to life, with this dance.

"Get rid of whatever you saw down there," he whispered. "It's over now."

She wanted to tell him, "I am hollow. I have no tears. I have no eggs. My womb is empty."

Dionisio's brow was lined. His face had aged, even in the brief time she had been up here with him. He hardly ever slept.

He was always at her bedside, gazing at her, trying to bring her back. She thought of the place she had come from, the man who had given her life. Had that man ever danced like this, with a woman in his arms, had he ever loved like this? Yes, once. Estrella. The woman whom the thing had been made to imitate.

As the Calliope creature let Dionisio dance her around the room, she thought of Doctor. He was the only one who could understand her hollowness—he who had become mechanical with grief.

She could feel the real Calliope calling her, summoning her down. That was where she belonged. And the real Calliope should be here dancing with her lover, full of their child, making green plants rise up from the earth everywhere she stepped.

PAUL'S LETTER

Dear Rafe,

I hope this letter finds you. I've sent it with the Old Clown who finally chose the desert over Under. As the days pass, I can't say I blame him. I have dreams of those women bursting into flames. Their ghosts call me down.

What is it like where you are? I've almost gone after you so many times. But then something stops me. I don't know if it's my inability to give up Elysia or my fear that when I see you I will lose myself. I realize now that the main reason I let you go—encouraged you (did I?)—was my fear that my love for you was too strong. I thought I needed to become complete, less needy, in order to be able to love. Of course, I also feared for your safety if you stayed here, but I could have gone with you, even convinced Calliope and Dionisio to come; I see that now. But my head scorned my heart, and now my heart won't let my head rest for a moment.

I had wanted to wait to write to you until Calliope had her child. Yes, she is pregnant. We found out right after you left. I thought that when the baby was born we might all be strong enough to go after you. But something has happened. I hesitate to tell you because I don't want you to worry, but I think you should know. Callie went Under. She had one of her ideas about finding some kind of magic to green the desert, so she went down looking for your father. She's back with us now, but something is wrong with her. She hardly speaks and she is very cold. Also, there are no signs of life inside her.

Rafe, I don't want you to do anything yet. I don't think it would be wise for you to come back here now. I'm not sure what your father is capable of. But as soon as Callie is better—we are going to get her better—we will come to find you. Whatever it takes, Rafe.

Paul

RESCUE MISSION

Like a rescue let me hold you
My limbs can be the ladder
Let me hold you like a rescue
My eyes can be the candles
Lead you from the castle

Like a rescue let me hold you
Let me hold you like a rescue
Till we reach our destination
Till we reach the rescue mission

Release the pain you hold within
With the veins that rope my hands
Take the flower's secret stamen
To create regeneration
We will leave behind bone chambers
We'll escape our blood-stained visions
Cross the deserts of destruction
Till we reach our destination
Till we reach the rescue mission

Like a rescue let me hold you
My limbs can be the ladder
Let me hold you like a rescue
My eyes can be the candles
Lead you from the castle

Like a rescue let me hold you
Let me hold you like a rescue
Till we reach our destination
Till we reach the rescue mission

There beneath the spilling fountains
Water lilies light like lanterns
In a maze of secret gardens
Where our songs grow on the branches
From the clouds the golden chalice
Rains the shower and the dove
On the water lilies glisten
All our sorrows turned to . . .

If my body is your freedom
Then you will rescue me
If my body is your safety
Then you will set me free

We will leave these stone chill chambers
For illuminated gardens
Cross the water lilies pavement
Beneath skies of golden goblets
And you stand in your dark garden
Where you've planted work of lifetimes
And your thoughts will blossom gold
Shower down upon the world

Like a rescue let me hold you
Let me hold you like a rescue
Till we reach our destination
Till we reach the rescue mission
We will reach the rescue mission

Set each other free

Rescue Mission 3

Calliope sat in the darkness with Primavera in her arms. She was pretending that the train was in motion, taking her and her daughter through the landscape of old ones and ash-addicts, the sick-rooms and the temples of bars where the only gods were drugs. The conductor would come walking down the aisle, swinging with the motion of the train. He would have plum-black curls and a wild sweetness in his face.

She would cry his name and he would embrace her, kiss her child. His child. Dionisio.

"We are going up," he would say. "Next stop Elysia, baby-girls."

The train door slid open, the gate of metal on metal, and

Calliope jumped, half-expecting her lover to be standing there in the darkness.

But no, it must be the real conductor of this motionless train, she thought. My father.

It was not her father. The figure stepped forward. It was Calliope.

Calliope gasped as the face that was just like her own watched her with those glassy eyes.

"Why are you here?" she asked the creature. She remembered the vision of her lover holding this thing. Had it come for Primavera? Trembling, she held her child against her breast. "You can't have her."

The Calliope thing stared at Primavera. Then she touched her own abdomen, wincing as if in pain.

But she can't experience pain, Calliope thought. She doesn't know pain.

"I don't want to take her," the creature said in a voice so like Calliope's own that Primavera turned her downy head as if confused and made a soft, bleating sound. "I know she's yours. And his. I can never make a child."

"Why are you here?" Calliope cried again.

"No," said the thing that had stolen Calliope's face. "That is not why."

"What?"

"They changed me."

"Who?"

"I am almost a real woman now."

Calliope felt fear welling in her throat. She imagined this thing clutching Primavera, going back up to Dionisio and Paul, born. And she, Calliope, left behind, discarded like the cocoon.

"You can't have her."

"No," the creature said.

She is more beautiful than I am, Calliope thought. She is younger than I am. Already, I am more carved by time. She will be young forever.

The thing came closer, holding out her hands. Primavera looked at her and smiled with delight, reached out.

Even my own daughter doesn't know, Calliope thought. This is only a nightmare, a hallucination, she told herself. I am broken.

But would she ever wake up, come to, repair?

"You have my lover, my friend, my music, my home, my life," she said. "Not my child, too."

She turned, hearing the sound of footsteps. Doctor was coming. The creature opened the train door.

"Hurry," it said.

"What?"

"I am not like you. How can I pretend? They need you. Their love is so strong. It almost made a mechanical heart pump blood."

The footsteps were nearer.

"Go quickly."

Calliope staggered toward the door. She was shaking so much that Primavera seemed to tremble also.

"Calliope," Doctor called.

"Hurry. Go quickly. I can pretend I'm you until you get away."

Calliope looked at the thing that wore her face. Who was this that had entered her life, lived her life, and then come down to rescue her? Who was this soulless thing that had found a soul, only to give up the life that had given it that soul? What was Calliope leaving behind underground as she returned to her loved ones with her daughter? Always, for eternity, the Calliope creature would remain Under, unchanged like a mummy that chattered and danced.

"Go," it said.

Calliope pressed her daughter to her chest and ran out of the subway car into the perpetual night.

The other Calliope stayed behind. When Doctor came looking for his daughter, the creature held out her arms to him. He knew her immediately, but he did not run after the real Calliope and Primavera. He was mesmerized by the sight of his creation.

"You came back," he said, his voice catching in his throat. He stumbled.

She nodded stiffly. Her smile was so perfect, her flesh, if it could be called flesh, unlined. "I belong here," she said. "With you."

He remembered Estrella. Estrella had never said those words to him. She had said, "Come with me away from here," begging him to leave the desert. Then she had let him go down alone, underground.

This creature he had made looked like Estrella. He had given her everything—life itself, and then Elysia's beauty and the chance to live in it forever. But she had come back down.

He began to cough.

"We are the same," the creature was saying. "We are the same."

No, he thought, not the same. You will remain.

The withered man collapsed. The creature took him in her arms, let his head rest in her lap. There was an avalanche inside his chest—his stone heart splitting, crushed into billowing clouds of dust which rose to choke him, blocked his veins. He was wandering into the desert, becoming the desert. He should never have left it.

Now his body would become the soil out of which his grand-daughter's oasis garden would grow.

And the old ones were stirring—dreaming of a black-haired boy leading them up from Under into that garden.

CALLIOPE

We take only what we can easily carry—thin sheaths and blanket cloaks, some utensils and tools, our instruments—and put everything into the car. We leave the loft just as it is with the garden mural and the tapestry cushions, the velvets and im-itation flowers. We do not even lock the doors.

Paul is driving and Dionisio sits beside him. I am in the back with Primavera.

It is night. We are silent as we drive down the cobblestone

streets. This city is like the colors when rainwater mixes with oil in gutters. Abalone iridescence shining on the surface of the dark.

In the windows of bars, we see mechanical dolls serving parfaits and exotic drinks with parasols to the beautiful children. Primavera reaches out her arms to the lights, the faces blurred behind lit, misty glass. But she does not cry when we do not stop. Perhaps she is not wishing to remain but giving them a blessing.

Suddenly, we are at the end of Elysia. Like an island or a city on the edge of a cliff, like a city on a cloud, it is suddenly over. We pass breathless into the darkness, half-expecting to vanish. Dionisio reaches for my knee from the front seat, and I touch Paul's shoulder with my hand; my daughter holds on to me. She is warm and firm and smells of pollen. We are all still here.

I remember how I ran out into the dunes once, as a child, searching for Rafe. I had this same sensation then, even more powerfully. I got out of the car; there was nothing to protect me from the vast, untamed night. How could my brother have come here alone? I wondered. Nothing but his disappearance could have brought me out into this.

Now I am driving into this desert by choice. I am bringing my child with me. As if I am not afraid.

The car headlights illuminate rows of cactus. They look like crippled bodies of the ones who go Under. Maybe they are the spirits of the old ones who refused to go below and wandered into this desert. Unlike the ones Under, they do not have to wear the faces of their dead bodies forever. They can be fleshy, spined desert children. This is freedom, I think. Maybe these trees dance when no one is here to see. Maybe their spikes turn to blossoms.

The car charges over the sand. Paul begins to sing: "Till we reach our destination/We will reach the rescue mission." His voice sounds like the song of the desert itself—ancient, haunted, full of secret tears.

Suddenly, Paul stops singing. "Will we find him, Callie?" he asks me, and I touch his shoulder again, point across the dunes to where I know Rafe lives now.

"When I first met him, I knew how he would look asleep," Paul says. "Isn't that strange? That's the closest I've come to one of Calliope's visions."

Paul sounds different, I think. His voice is softer than I have ever heard it.

I close my eyes, trying to bring back last night's vision. "I saw something," I say. "I saw us returning to release the old ones. And he was with us. I think it was him. I couldn't see his face."

I feel the tension in Paul's shoulders ease a little. Primavera opens her arms and reaches for her father.

"You're so serious," Dionisio says to her. "Like she's planning the way it is going to look."

"Maybe that's what she's doing," I say.

"What will it look like, Primavera?" Paul asks her. "Will there be rivers and trees and flowers? Do you see our oasis?"

Primavera laughs as if she knows exactly what he is saying to her.

And we keep driving, toward the green that our daughter sees.

RAFE'S DESERT SONG

My drums, make trees dance
My drums, make leaves dance
My drums, make flames dance

My drums, be the heart
of this Old One
whose face has become
withered and wise in the fields of the sun

My drums, be the heart
of this Old One
who sings of his scars
points up above and can name all the stars

My drums, be the children's feet as they dance

My drums, make songs come
We are all one
As each life ends
New life has begun
My drums, be the water, earth, air, and sun.

Desert Song 4

*R*afe gazed across the parched, sunset-colored sand. The twisted cactus cast no shadow. No mirage of three musicians playing in a garden appeared on the horizon. Although Rafe wished for such a vision.

Some nights, before bedtime, sitting by the fire, he told the desert children about Calliope's premonitions, Paul's voice, Dionisio's music. But time was passing. They were no longer so real to him. In their room of murals and tapestry, they were like enchanted creatures from a tale. Even their beauty—Calliope's long, glossy hair wreathed in silk flowers, Paul's molten aura, Dionisio's wine-stained, almost feminine lips and wine-bright eyes—even these things were enchantments, not real, not part of this real world of dust and toil.

Rafe had accepted the desert. He no longer dreamed of

driving back to Elysia. This was his home now. He loved the old men and women with their lines and their stories of lost worlds. He loved the skinny, ragged children who followed him everywhere as he did his tasks. They were always hungry for fruits, vegetables, grains, thirsty for fountains, pools, lakes, weary from endless working, but they had mothers, fathers, grandparents, brothers, and sisters wherever they looked. And they would grow old like this, cherished, no matter how time made them stoop or crumple.

If only I could give them the paradise they see trembling in waves of hallucinatory heat along the horizon, Rafe thought. And if it were real, maybe Calliope, Dionisio, and Paul would come. Because even if his family had become a fairy tale, even though he wondered, sometimes, if he had made up that other life, still he yearned for it. When he saw the desert children staring, hypnotized, at their mirages—that is what it was like when he thought of his family. They were the world he wanted, finally, to immerse himself in, the water that would soothe his throat, the trees that would shelter him from relentless sun. A child could look away from his mirage and go back to work, not try to run after his vision. He knew that it was out of reach, but the sorrow of not being able to touch it always haunted him. In the same way, Rafe remembered.

Rafe's hands pattered on the drum he held between his knees. Drops of sound.

And that was when the thunder cracked.

He lifted his face, opened his mouth. Was he crying? A scent of sage rose up—green and distilled. It was almost a burning smell as the pure rain touched the scorched earth.

Still drumming, he scrambled down the warm rocks to the meeting grounds. Everyone had gathered, dancing in circles, holding up their buckets to the sky. Sun-and-wind-weathered men and women, barefoot, dusty children. They sang the sun to sleep, watching the rainbow flashes it left behind for them like its dreams. They sang the huge round gold moon up into the wet sky.

"Rafe."

He felt a hand on his shoulder and turned to see an old man, a traveler probably; Rafe didn't recognize him at first.

"Yes."

"I have a message for you," the man said. "From Elysia."

It was the Old Clown without costume or makeup, dressed in ancient leather and dust.

"You left," Rafe said.

"I thought I might as well die out here as there. And this needed to be delivered."

He handed the crumpled envelope over. Rafe's heart pounded. He looked at the man's mapped face, following the roads of lines. Roads that could bring people away from their carousels and Ferris wheels. Roads that could bring people here, to the sage and the stars.

"Thank you."

"It might be old news," the man said. "I've had a rough journey. Car broke down and I was at an outpost for weeks."

Rafe ripped open the envelope, tearing the note inside. As he held the pieces together to read them, he recognized Paul's writing. Rain made the letters bleed.

"We will come to find you," the letters said.

As soon as the storm ended, the thirsty earth was dry. Everyone made their beds on the dry sand in the circle of candlelight. Only the air retained some of the moisture. The people drank it in their sleep.

Rafe wandered alone with his drum, down among the rocks to a ravine. By the edge of this bed of sand squatted the huge stone man. Rafe sat beside him.

Is this what I will become out here? he thought, his hand on the man's flank. Will I become stone? How could I have left them? He took the pocket watch from Estrella out of his shirt. The tiny clock in the shape of a drum had long since stopped running.

"Please, Calliope," he whispered, "fight off whatever chases you. Use all your powers. I'll be there soon."

He would get in his car when it was light and head back to his family. Why had he ever left them at all? What did it matter how long he lived, out here in the desert, if he lived without them?

Then Rafe heard the trickle and saw the moonlit sheen at the bottom of the ravine. Somehow the earth had not swallowed this glaze of water; now it shone like a light, like a star river, quenching the stone man, beckoning to travelers.

He thought he felt a flutter of wings brush the air—twin petals in flight.

"Lily." The memory of her was suddenly so palpable—different from an Orpheus vision; she was less distinct but somehow more a part of him. They shared a heartbeat and a voice.

"The desert will green," she was saying. "Play, Rafe. Make it."

He lowered his head and began to play his drum. And the rain fell again.

It was a gentle rain that did not even wake the people sleeping beyond the rocks. They smiled as clear drops slid down their cheeks and into their mouths.

Rafe did not know how long he played. His hands ached. The rain made a curtain around him, separating him from everything like a liquid forest. When he finally looked up from his drums it was morning. As the sun touched the raindrops like a painter, colors materialized, half blinding him. He squinted, looking out across the ravine that was full of rushing water.

On the other side, where there had only been sand and rocks, there was now a garden.

Fountains like crystal trees merging with the rain, real trees covered with fruits, green banks where birds with rainbow plumage paraded, pools where swans so white they were silver floated, sleek black and white horses grazing among flowers that looked like what flowers might dream of when they shut their petals. And on this garden stage beneath a leafy canopy, a dark man played his bass, its power resonating from his hips, a blond man's guitar caught the light, electric flashes from his mind to his hand, a woman made her keyboards sing the rhythms beneath her breast. The child at the woman's feet wore so many blossoms that she looked more like a flower spirit than a human child. Ecstasia.

This was not a mirage.

> *Release the pain you hold within*
> *With the veins that rope my hands*
> *Take the flower's secret stamen*
> *To create regeneration*
> *We will leave behind bone chambers*
> *We'll escape our blood-stained visions*
> *Cross the deserts of destruction*
> *Till we reach our destination*
> *Till we reach the rescue mission*

Still playing his drum, Rafe waded through the water to meet them.